To So

Best Wishes:

Tom Scilipoti

Up All Night

Tom Scilipoti

PublishAmerica
Baltimore

First printing

At the specific preference of the author, PublishAmerica allowed this work to remain exactly as the author intended, verbatim, without editorial input.

ISBN: 1-4241-7102-4
PUBLISHED BY PUBLISHAMERICA, LLLP
www.publishamerica.com
Baltimore

Printed in the United States of America

Dedication

To my parents, who read to me when I was little.

Acknowledgments

I never could have imagined publishing a novel before graduating from college. This was my mistake—I failed to realize that it would take me four and half years to graduate from college. Just kidding, but not really. No I failed to realize how many great people there were surrounding me and how instrumental they would be to my growth as a writer. In fact, I can say with confidence that without the numerous individuals (too many to name) that have encouraged, inspired, educated, entertained, challenged, and motivated me over the years, this book would never be in your hands. So for these people I am eternally grateful. Although everyone I've known has had some effect on my growth as a writer, there are some particular people I'd like to recognize.

From the John Carroll School I'd like to recognize Mr. Matthew Scott Blair—"What's up Fool?". Mr. Paul Barker, whose wisdom helped bring me back to the faith. Mrs. Anne Klarich, who believed in my talent from my days as an annoying high school freshman. And especially Mr. Mark Ionescu, who was more than a teacher.

From Gettysburg College—Dr. Lou Hammann, who helped served as an academic role model for my sophomoric self. Dr. Paula Olinger, who encouraged my unique ways. Dr. Bill Jones, who helped me see the light. And especially Mrs. Sheila Mulligan, whose unselfish aid will not go unremembered.

From the beach summers—I don't know where to start. I guess I can thank Officer Christine Plant from the OCPD for teaching me, "You Ain't 21, You ain't drinkin." That was an invaluable lesson as well as the gospel truth. I can thank John Cunningham for motivating me to defend my beliefs. John Davis for being "aight". Adam Hagelin for making me laugh. Dave Ivy for his critical help, insight, and friendship. Matt Ullman, for inspiring a legendary glutton fest at a local McDonald's on late August night. Ryan Peusch for teaching me to believe in my self. Christian Kansler for inspiring me to succeed. Ryan Gauthier for helping me to see the world with new eyes. Christine Lakin, for inspiring me to be a good person. And, because I know she'll get upset if I don't mention her name, Meghan Marchiano, for listening and being a good friend.

I'd also like to thank Mrs. Mary Jean-Craig for inspiring the book idea. Nick Van Horn and Adam Trionfo for their philosophical company as well as funny and faithful friendship. Mrs. Susan and Mr. Chris Trionfo, for welcoming me into their home, their hearts, and illuminating the Christian Path.

And finally, I'd like to thank my parents, my brother, and my extended family. Mom, Dad—you read to me when I was little and I couldn't have asked for better parents. Dad—you'll always be my role model and Mom—you'll always be closest to my heart. Tony, whether you realize it or not, there's a lot I've learned from you. And Dupey, Pop, the faithful departed, the Komenda and Scilipoti families—remember that this book is technically fiction so any thing that happens may or may not be historically true but the key lesson—the importance of loving your family and friends, that is certainly is non-fiction.

Tom Scilipoti
Gettysburg College
February 1st, 2007

Table of Contents

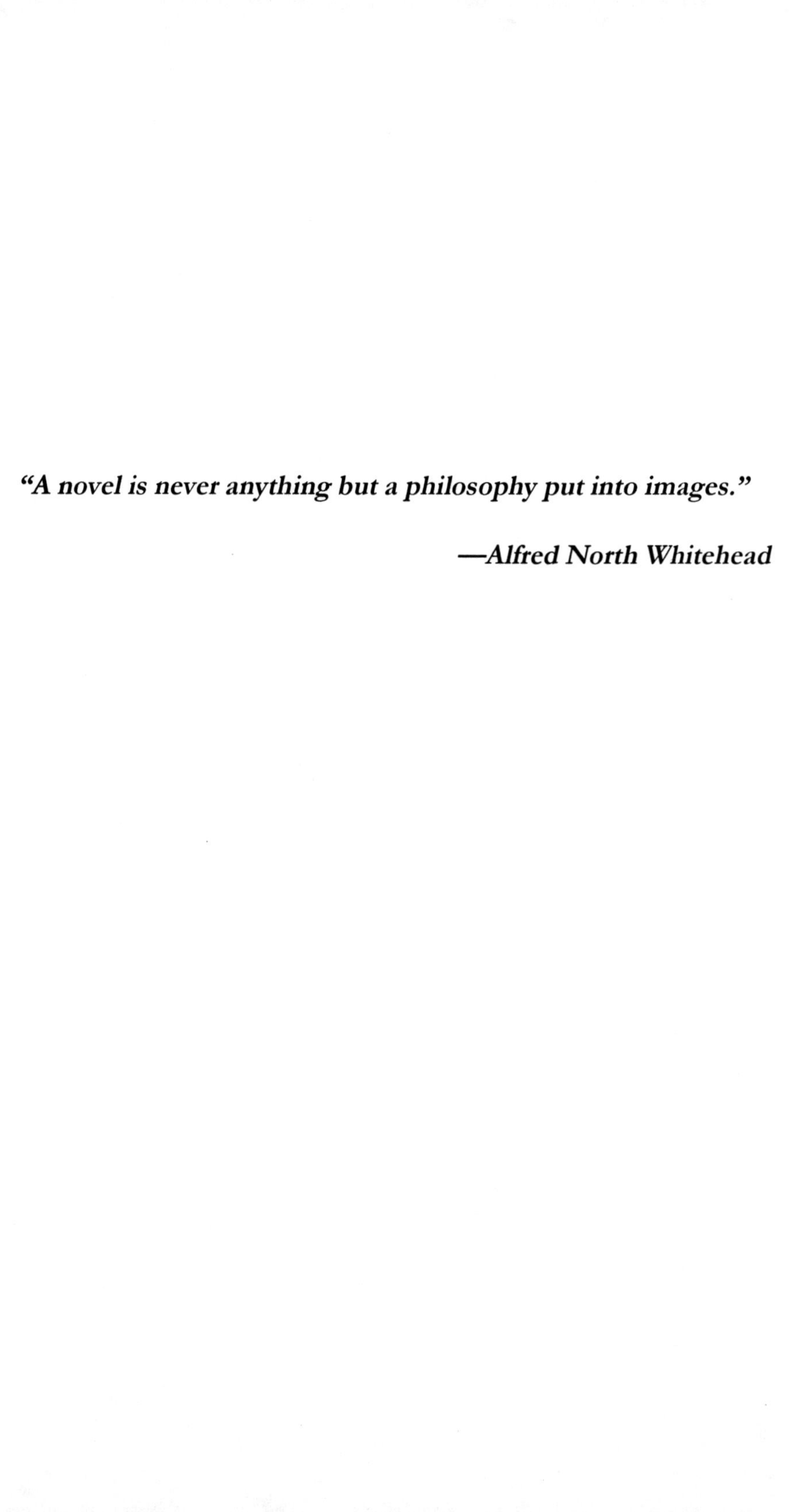

"A novel is never anything but a philosophy put into images."

—Alfred North Whitehead

Wake

"I want to know God's thoughts; the rest are details"—Einstein

'What if Jesus was really coming back soon?

The world seems to be growing only more chaotic everyday and there's no better time like the present for a return. If he came back would he really destroy the earth like the Scripture says?

And would heaven and earth become one?

On what grounds would he judge people?

On blind faith?

On Good Works?

On size of heart?

And would I be worthy of ascension by his standards?

What would he look like and would people even believe in his message?

What would he say to the world?

Does the fact that he has yet to return prove he wasn't divine and the post-Easter tradition, a big hoax?

What if he never existed and the Christian faith was an elaborate sham?

Or what if he was among us and we just didn't know it?

What if Gandhi was really the 2nd coming?

What if Christ incarnates in every honest Christian?

What if he was only a prophet?

What if he was just a poor peasant that happened to be highly intelligent, enlightened, and decided to preach a new law in his early 30's—unconditional love regardless of social class or health status?"

were all honest questions that rose from the depths of my soul, beyond my control, all the way to the center of my mental universe in concert with choir of confusing childhood memories of Christmas Catholics confidently chanting, "Christ has died, Christ has risen, Christ will come again."

It was 3 a.m. in mid-July and I wanted go to bed. I had the deepest of metaphysical questions running through my head. I was out patience, looking for a night sleep as I had been up all night for the third night in a row. My mind was sinking into a frenzy of epistemological confusion and a great flight from the MTV generated life was being launched. The curiosity of what philosophers call "the human condition" fused with a mysterious change in mind was the catalyst. As a result, the innocent, comfortable life I once knew had now died. My confusion had risen. And the sleepless nights would come again. This much I had faith in.

Deep down, I didn't feel like my usual self but why exactly I felt this way I couldn't be certain. At the time, I just attributed the sublime change in mood to some kind of spiritual growth or early enlightenment. Such was my rational explanation, for now. And only because I had a rational explanation, did I let myself continue to puzzle over life's most potent mysteries for the duration of the endless night.

"Why do bad things happen to good people?
What's the meaning of life?
What's it feel like to be in love?
Will I ever find a girl?
Is there one true religion?
What happens when we die?
Do good people go to heaven?
If they don't then is there any incentive for being good and does life still have a purpose?
If they do how do we get there, what is it like, and where is it located?
Is faith in Jesus the ticket to heaven?

Was Jesus really God's son or just a messenger of Truth?
Why was he rejected by so many Jewish people?
Can I get to heaven without him?
Should I accept him as teacher or personal Lord and savior?
What was the real message of the Gospels?
On which principles should I shape my life?
If it feels good do it?
Love your neighbor as yourself?
Submit to Christ?
Treat women like angels?
Treat women like horny human beings and fulfill their desires?
Follow the 8 fold path?
Observe the 10 commandments?
Listen to the wind of my soul?"

My moments of heavy meditation did subside, thankfully, with the onset of daylight. Because they did, I returned to more common, concrete thinking in tune with the rising sun. When I did, I quickly said a timely prayer—"Dear Lord, help me get some sleep."

I hoped, in this prayerful period, that I could eventually imitate my roommates—high school classmates from The Meister Eckhart School in Bel Air, MD, who all knew the secrets to sound sleep. These were secrets that I should have sought to apply in light of my burning insomnia.

One of my sleeping roommates from our three story apartment complex known by Beach City locals as "The Pink Palace" was John Garfield. A film student at Art Institute of New York, John had learned the ways of the world from endless pot smoking sessions in front of the screen. He could quote any major movie made in the last ten years as well as smoke two packs of cigs without coming up for air. His secret to sound sleep was eighteen beers, a couple bong hits, some Pizza Tugos, and then he was out. Then there were Peter Darwin and Mark Locke. They lived in the room across the hall.

Peter was Pre-Med at the University of Virginia and had a masterful grasp of classic American literature for his young age. Mark was a business major at Roanoke College and owner of the most accurate Ruit—drinking game of skill and ping pong ball throwing (beer pong), stroke in the entire city. Peter and Mark had recipes for sound sleep similar to John with the exception that theirs usually included girls. Peter's sleep aid was his girlfriend Kelly, Mark's was usually a random high school girl.

Regardless of their secrets, however, all of my roommates passed out with ease each and every evening with big smiles on their flushed faces. I used to snooze every night this summer like them, but recently I had been experiencing serious pain in my kidneys. Now, I'm not a doctor—far from it, I am a philosophy major from Sacred Heart College, but I'm pretty sure the pain had something to do with the fact that I had been drinking excess amounts of keg beer everyday for the last two months. Regardless of the source though, I had stopped binge drinking recently and now found my self in a fierce battle with sleeplessness.

When my uncle called at 9 a.m., I was still awake and unwell despite the simpler direction of my thoughts.

"Listen Chris. I'm comin down to your place to fix your car, dude. Is that killer or what? Then we're gonna go out to Happy Jacks' and eat pancakes and shit," my uncle informed me.

"Um that sounds good. Umm, it sounds real good. It sounds great actually. Really great." I responded in an unenthused, courtesy tone. I didn't want breakfast—I wanted sleep.

For all of my ailments though, I thought I could see glimpses of God's glory. It was morning, I was sleepless, and my uncle Joe, a reformed drug addict as well as the source of the glimpses, was pretty inspirational.

My uncle Joe drove two hundred miles from my hometown—Bel Air, MD, despite his busy schedule to Beach City with the sole intention of fixing my car and taking me out to breakfast. In the face of his previous troubles with the all too human problem of addiction, he still thanked the Good Lord his health, happiness and family. Therefore, my uncle truly inspired me as his faith had triumphed over the destructive lure of drug use.

Literally speaking, my uncle Joe fixed my car—a car that my mother had loaned me, a Pink Cadillac, and then drove me to breakfast—a meal I hadn't eaten in months of Beach City living. The two of us ate a pancake breakfast and drank cold beers on the beach until he dropped me off at work on his way back to Bel Air. Figuratively speaking however, my uncle helped me begin to find my way back to God. I know this statement sounds odd, and it is, but the Lord does have a reputation for the mysterious way in which he works.

I was thinking about my uncle's transformation from drug addict to Good Samaritan when a path cleared. After I took a sip of my water at breakfast, I gazed around the room and noticed a framed biblical passage that hung on the restaurant wall.

> *"Create in me a clean heart, O God, and put a new and right spirit within me"*
> *-Psalm 51:10*

Instantly, I drew a profound sense of holiness from the passage. It seemed as though God were speaking directly to me—that I was being called to see this passage in the white light. I had been a drunken slob all summer and now the Lord was calling me out through this Psalm as he had done with my uncle Joe I figured.

As a result of the passage's power, my heart was pierced with divine love, my mind was lifted with ineffable joy, and my body was blessed with sublime chills. The moment was very unusual, way beyond verbal description in essence. But for the sake of my story, I will say that it started to give me a profound respect for the power of Hebrew scripture. It also helped fertilize the seeds of a change in mind from the everyday—girls, work, beer to the eternal—god, faith, destiny.

Discovery of this nature is obviously not ordinary life experience for a boy of summer who until recent kidney problems drank keg beer every single day without exception. It's not an everyday moment for an incoming college sophomore who until recent kidney problems did keg stands as if he had gills. It's not a routine occurrence for a blackout stoner who until recent sleep troubles never could turn down a marathon session of quarters, flip cup, and of course, Ruit despite the fact that he had to work the next morning. Therefore, I had to take a leap of faith and believe that my life was starting to change.

I had to believe that God was starting to create in me a clean heart and lead me to new life. That's the only way I could rationalize the intensity of insomnia and the ineffability of the psalm. I couldn't rationalize it in terms of bad brain chemistry. I had been very, very religious as a child, indifferent as a teen, and now God was calling be back. Such was my only explanation.

My friends were all waking up with chronic hangovers at this time, some with random girls in their bed, others with sand and piss, and a few, like Mark, had a combination of all three. I was, on the converse, awake from the night before. I was, on the converse, eating breakfast for the first time in months. I was, on the converse, listening for a celestial calling. The polarity of our present was astronomical but rightfully so. I was now, thanks to the sudden sleeplessness and soul search to follow, on a mission—a mission rooted in reaching out for answers to "those questions the heart asks but the head can't answer" to borrow a term from Needleman. My friends, on the contrary, were on a 45-day booze binge, searching passionately for skuzzers—girls you call up when you want to get laid, and looney bin pot only.

Clearly, the foundations now were in place for the titanic clashes of worldview and Grecian dramas that would eventually unfold over the latter part of this summer. For now though, peace and harmony were still the norms and going to the beach with my uncle was still my first instinct.

After breakfast I acted on that instinct by asking my uncle Joe to drive us to the dunes. "Sure dude. Anything you want, my little buddy," my uncle replied after my inquiry. "But let's get a couple cold Natty Boh's first," he followed.

Shortly thereafter we *peace rolled* to the sands, and quickly arrived on the 39th street dunes illegally packing a twelve pack of Natty Boh. The beautiful weather that we were graced with—97, clear and sunny, gradually alleviated my mood from cracked out-tired to vibrant-awake and I genuinely felt an Emersonian appreciation for this therapeutic quality of Nature.

Now gazing awestruck into the religious reflection of the golden sun that illuminated the ocean waters, I slowly began to forget about my intense night of curious contemplation. The mysteries of faith were, like I now considered them to be as I glimmered in the scorching summer sun, *mysteries* and therefore better left unsolved. God was ultimately real and I just had to trust in his providence as I now saw it with a cool beer buzz. And so, metaphysics and mysteries finally exiting my waning mind, I sat back and defiantly devoured cold National Bohemian beers on the beach sands.

"Dude Chris, man. You ever watch the history channel? There's some cool shit on there. I was watching this thing on the Greeks. They were really f-in smart," my uncle informed me.

"Yeah they were. A lot of our best ideas come from the Greeks—philosophy, geometry, democracy." I responded with confidence.

"Yeah dude. This guy Aristotle. He did everything. He studied like zoology, physics, philosophy, chemistry. Started schools. Tutored Alexander the great. F-in smart," my uncle followed just before my roommate Mark walked out on the beach.

"What's up boy-eee?" My uncle asked Mark upon his sun-glassed shaggy blonde haired arrival.

"Just came out to catch some waves." Mark replied.

"Killer" my uncle answered. "You guys are some lucky sons of bitches," he followed.

'Trust me—we know." I responded.

"Mark let's chill, dude. Let's drink some beers." I followed peacefully.

"You're not allowed to drink on the beach." Mark said as if "thou shall not drink on the beach" were the 11th commandment.

"If you follow all of the rules, you'll miss of the fun Mark. And that's a really lame rule anyway. Our parents don't even follow it." I answered.

"Whatever dude. I gotta work in an hour." Mark replied.

"Alright, bro." I followed.

So my uncle Joe and I sat on the beach in direct defiance of Neo-Prohibition oriented local law while Mark body boarded. We shared laughs and drank cold Boh's in the sun as if neither Standard Eastern Time nor the threat of legal penalty could hinder us in our pursuit of happiness. This acquired taste of liberation, as a result, was both delicious and soothing like a glass of cold water after a long day of labor in the sun.

As 3:30 p.m. struck, however, that smooth taste turned flat. Like 99.999% of the world, I had to work to survive. Accepting the bitter reality that I had to do so in a half hour for minimum wage in a superficially slanted business set in, sending my good mood southward.

The heavy religiosity that the foggy night spawned would not mix well with the money crazed business I worked at. And I knew this. I had been fine since breakfast because I was with one of my favorite uncle's and having a good time on the beach. But now I was headed to the Roller Dough—a place I was very frustrated with.

Most of the waitresses I had to associate myself with were so obsessed with themselves that I'm pretty sure if I died on the job, they probably wouldn't even notice. Also, the boss mistook my kindness for weakness and always made me do random chores. And then she laughed about it. I just felt like Milton from Office Space at the Roller Dough but today, empowered by the Spirit, I would have no more of this nonsense.

So instead of putting on uniform, I wore what I wanted to wear to work as an ode to Office Space—my favorite film. I figured that as long as I did my job properly that it didn't matter what wore. Especially because I was making minimum wage and knew I wasn't going to be serving tables today. So I wore what I wanted to wear to work—Meister Eckhart soccer jersey, flowered shorts, and sandals, and hopped into my Uncle's big, green truck with the winds starting to blow mightily—a storm was coming.

As my uncle Joe drove me to the Roller Dough, the storm finally hit. A safe summer sunshine had become a furious torrential downpour—the most furious I had seen this summer, in a matter of minutes. It was a situation that was rich in symbolism.

I really was suffering from insomnia as well as struggling to find resolutions to my deep, religious inquiries. As a result, my brain chemistry was slightly abnormal and my spirit had a mysterious God-oriented pull. The symbolism of the storm made a lot of sense and paralleled my mood. Therefore, I saw heavy metaphors in the rainstorm.

Growing wide-eyed and unwell with the flooding streets, I started to think of Noah and the Great Flood. Sleep deprived and anthropomorphically tilted, I wondered ominously if the furious storm cast on Beach City was really just God cleansing a city contaminated with sin—the city had been nothing but one to me ever since I sobered up.

After observing six straight rounds of Senior Week, I reached one conclusion and one conclusion only—everybody my age that came to Beach City just wanted instant pleasure and nothing more. And I say that as a very sympathetic euphemism. The cultural trend was to forget about God, forget about living with meaning, and submit yourself solely to booze, drugs, and a finally a random fill for the night cap. So this rainstorm, in a poetic sense, was God bearing his judgment on his lost children as I saw it.

When we reached my workplace on 70th street, I gave my uncle Joe a reluctant "goodbye" like a child would give when his mother drops him off at a bad babysitter's house. Despite my initial worry however, I walked proudly into work, right on time and completely out of proper uniform.

Mark, quickly after seeing my awesome attire said, "You can't wear sandals to work! Why the hell are you wearing that?"

"To prove a point," I answered. "That my presence is more important than my attire."

"Ew, what is that weirdo doing?" Kim, one of the waitresses asked her fellow waitress Alecia. "Why is he talking like that and why is he wearing sandals?" She followed.

"Chris, this is my restaurant, you do as I say! Go home and change! This is why you'll never be a waiter," my boss informed me.

"No, I'll never be a waiter because you need me to be your minimum wage making bitch," I thought.

Obedient, optimistic, but definitely not my usual self, I walked thirty one streets back home in a fury of rainfall. I didn't mind because not only did I feel out of my body, which made me feel high—like I was slapping fives with angels, but I also had the pleasure of seeing first hand in a symbolically coded sense—"Dues Ex Machina" or God in the Machine. This was a term used in literature to describe moments when God—the eternal, stepped into the finite world of creation to teach people a lesson. In this case, God was Nature, Beach City traffic was the Machine, and the lesson would be about the beauty of forgiveness.

I was starting to change at a furious pace. A storm was raging not only outside me, but more importantly inside of me. Awareness of the divine was never even a dream in these last four seasons of keg stands and booting rallies. But the times were changing, and I was becoming more like a Hebrew tribesman with the passing minutes.

Figuratively, I saw the rain as a gift from the heavens just like our ancient ancestors had. I admired its cleansing quality and danced merrily in the puddles like a small child during my most joyous moments of insight.

I started to learn, in this inspirational moment, how not to shape my young life by observing the machine of angry beachgoers who all made the classic mistake of trying to resist Nature. These tourists, the majority of them from Pennsylvania, drove as fast as they could through the flooded streets in hope of reaching their lifeless destinations fifteen seconds faster. Like the majority of modern-worlders, these Sketchslyvannians all made the fundamental mistake of prioritizing their time over their safety. Such behavior, reflective of our fast-paced culture, upset my stomach.

Instead of worrying about the potential $3 I was losing by walking home in the rain and not working, I just smiled and let the rainfall evoke childhood memories of playing in the rain. Time and money weren't my top concerns—just harmony.

As a result of my counter-culturally inclined view, "The unexamined life is not worth living," was my final thought, borrowed from Socrates and inspired from the chaos on Coastal Highway as I reached my home on 39th street following the two mile walk.

Without much hurry, I drank a few of the left over Natty Bohs, changed my comfortable clothes and walked back to 70th wearing the gradually soaking wet Roller Dough shirt that I had to pay $15 for. When I finally returned to the Roller Dough—the poor man's Pizza Hut, chaos was cooking in a literal sense. The American cooks had threatened to quit permanently if the Russian expeditors kept screwing up orders—a collective act which would surely instill chaos.

"If you bitches fuck up one more order…one more fucking order! We're all out of here." I heard Andy, the head cook, shout as I strolled to my expedition zone.

To add to the growing madness, The Boss ran around screaming like she was having a tantrum I previously thought would be characteristic only of a terrible two year old.

"Moooove! Get the fuck out of my way!" Missy screamed as she pushed her way past my former rugby playing, 5'8 215 pound body. Missy the Boss, as I later found out, had Bipolar Disorder and frequently went off her meds.

Every character I observed in my hazy state was rushing to make money by serving as many costumers as possible as it was the Roller Dough ideal. The Roller Dough "ideal", in my confirmed Roman Catholic mind, was an "ideal" driven by greed as quality service was consistently compromised for speed. Therefore it was a material "ideal" that I objected to with my conscience.

So I, the only American expeditor, grew a pair of testicles and became an instrument of peace. I worked like a 50's man to ensure that no more orders would be ruined, the frenzied pace would slow, and quality service would once again stay the sovereign practice.

As a result, I quickly became the quarterback of the Roller Dough calling all of the plays and proving to be somewhat successful. The cooks inevitably eased their threats after my intervention and the orders started to transfer smoothly from the greasy cooks to the easy waitresses.

The Boss though, had a slight problem with my success in making progress. This was *her* restaurant and although my presence was helpful see couldn't stand to sacrifice *her* authority for the greater good. Therefore, she tried to resist my Flutie-like efforts to quarterback. I tried to ignore her and continue to expedite orders but eventually I snapped and completely lost my patience because of a clueless waitress.

Instead of waiting her on her hungry tables, Alecia demanded to see the amount of money in credit card tips she had made that day. This act would require a decent chunk of time in addition to being irrelevant as staring at the digital figure wouldn't add to the total. But ultimately, the snap wasn't simply a result of Alecia's juvenile request. Rather it was a culmination of frustration with my superficial culture combined with a heavy streak of insomnia and a budding distaste for the Roller Dough ways. Even so, I diverted all of my bottled up anger onto this fellow employee.

"Shut the hell up Alecia and wait your God-damn tables. You'll see how much money you made when the shift is over. People are hungry and it's your job to serve them." I snapped to my co-worker.

"But I want to see how much money I made. I love money." Alecia responded.

"Money can't buy you happiness Alecia. You shouldn't love it. Just do your job well and your pay will follow." I answered.

"I love this kid. He's speaking like the Buddha." Adam, one of the only male servers added.

"Ugh, alright." Alecia replied very disappointedly.

Although Alecia probably deserved some of the diatribe, it was not like me to yell at people. But for the next six weeks, I couldn't always keep control. Part of the reason was the fact that I was undergoing a bio-chemically induced ecstasy but another part was existential. Everyone was so obsessed with sex, money, and external appearances that it seemed like no one ever slowed down to ponder what really gives life meaning. I did however, and in my special state of awareness felt free to evangelize my opinion.

"The Roller Dough sucks. I freakin' hate this place. I really do. It sucks. I've been getting paid minimum wage for six weeks for assistant managing. Assistant managing—doing everything. You promised that I would wait tables today and you broke your promise. I don't like promise breakers. They suck. So screw you I'm out of here!" I rapidly relayed to the Boss seconds before I gave a sarcastic wave to the waitresses as I left the Roller Dough, never to return.

The rain was still pouring down furiously on my walk home, but I didn't care. The rain that soaked me now meant forgiveness.

When I reached 39th the storm had finally mellowed, so my friends and I ran, wild at heart, out to the beach sands and chugged Natty Lights in the light drizzle.

"USA, USA, USA" we all shouted like we were imitating our childhood GI Joe's, appreciative of our residency—we currently lived not only in the greatest country in the world but also a governmentally sanctioned "All-American City" on Oceanside property. And I truly relished the moment like a big ole steak because I had waited so long to finally re-sample this tasty lifestyle of a nineteen year-old American boy—

one fortunate enough to be living Gatsby's dream on the beach sands before the onset of the Real World sun.

The rain finally stopped after we returned from the chugging session, the weather became a post-storm celestial shade, and so my friends and I all *peace rolled* to 73rd street to hangout with the beautiful eighteen year old beach girls in sublime skies. The weather was now tranquil, hence so was I. The post-rainfall sunset just soothed my soul with its placid rays and gave me an overwhelming sense of a natural forgiveness—a *sensus divinatatus* that Nature always forgives after unleashing her fury. Such was my final discovery.

Believing that my awakening was now finally over, I started to tell my magical story of rain and revelation on 73rd as if it were a tale from Genesis. My story had all the mystical elements of an early Biblical narrative in my view.

There was a moment of awakening to God. This moment occurred at breakfast when I got that unbelievably profound sense from looking at the biblical passage. There was an extraordinary voyage of discovery to follow. This was my experience of observing Dues ex Machina. Then finally, there was a truthful revelation—Nature always forgives after unleashing her fury. Therefore the story enchanted my friends.

My friend Jack, neighbor from the first floor's second unit as well as outspoken skeptic, was actually captivated by my story's power.

"That's the kind of story you could pass down to your kids." Jack told me with sincerity after hearing it from my converted lips.

Jack was a believer along with the majority of late teens who listened attentively. My neighbor from the first floor's first unit, Mary was especially accepting of my story.

A recent graduate of Hope High School, Mary Cooper was the epitome of a well-grounded, well-rounded human being. She was a volunteer for the Hope City Special Olympics and Red Cross chapter. She was a 4.0 student on an academic scholarship to Georgetown University. She was also a true believer and bleeding heart lover of both people and music.

"I believe your story Chris." Mary told me very faithfully.

"Thanks, Mary. It was inspired." I responded.

My roommate Peter, on the other hand, wasn't so convinced. He was very skeptical of my story.

"Apparently Chris had a revelation, where he doesn't care about money any more," he said to his girlfriend Kelly in a dangerously sarcastic tone.

Peter was a scientific mind and it didn't surprise me that he didn't believe in the Truth of my biblical experience. I didn't care about his uninspired skepticism though. I understood that not every universal truth could be fully grasped by human reason and that consequently, empirical sciences Peter studied, like psychology, had limits.

So despite Peter's sweeping pessimism, I continued to tell my tale for other accepting ears until I was rudely interrupted. Figuratively, I was interrupted by the superficial world represented by a late teen. Literally, I was interrupted a young lady who began to tell a depressing story of police corruption.

"So then it stopped raining and the weather cleared and the skies brightened and I felt like God was sending some kind of sign about forgive…"Something amazing just happened. You guys have to hear it, now!" The girl said as she barged in while I was at the end of telling my story.

"This cop just pulled us over and we had all this beer in the car. But then I started flirting with him and grabbed his dick so he let us go," she followed.

Instantly I felt a deep Puritan hatred for the story's sinful roots. It embodied everything that I despised about the gluttonous world I was born into—a world driven by lust, greed, corruption of power, indifference, and moral relativity, so I felt a "calling" to speak my mind to the confused teen but did so irrationally and without necessary compassion.

"You're a God-damn slut!" I asserted in all of my rage, translating my "snap of the finger" reaction to her story as party guests exploded in shock.

The gesture was pretty awesome and politically incorrect, but also very mean. However, I was a firm believer in the occasional value of uncensored honesty so I let stand for the time being. Later though, the saving grace of my conscience inspired me to participate in an apologetic reconciliation.

"Straighten up," she quickly instructed me, making a "straighten up" gesture—both arms in front of her face, parallel, shoulder width apart, with her arms to supplement her words.

"Straighten up?" I said. "That's ironic." I thought. "I'm usually a pretty decent, moral guy. She seems to be a superficially slanted skuzzer and *I'm* the one to straighten up? That's a reflection of our backwards culture."

I acted very impulsively, imitating the girl by running around the room yelling "straighten up, straighten up" and making the "straighten up" symbol that she flashed me earlier. Her reaction was legendary. She literally chased me around the room trying desperately to punch me square in the face.

The scene, as a result, was absolutely ridiculous—a conscientious objector trying to elude a MTV generated skuzzer's flying fists. Although I was laughing so hard that I could barely keep my balance, I did successfully dodge the young lady as she took a few passionate swings.

"Fuck you, I'm going to punch you in the fucking face," she kept screaming at me.

"Try and catch me, bitch." I shouted with glee.

Fortunately my roommate John intervened in our strange affair and eased the trouble.

"Dude, chill out," he said, sound advice from a stoner. "I'm trying to hook up with this girl later."

"Alright dude." I responded and stopped engaging this comedic situation out of respect for John's sex life.

Despite the running emotions on both sides of the feud, eventually reconciliation was attempted for the party was blessed with some "Good Christians".

Kelly, Hope High School classmate of my temporary adversary as well as a resident of 73rd, organized a dual apology and reconciliation. I eagerly participated because I understood both the poetic and practical quality of reconciling differences.

Under the request of her friend Kelly, my ideological counterpart soon gave me a forced "sorry" on her way out the door. Then she offered me a weak handshake. I however, denied the weak handshake and instead requested a hug because I thought a hug would be more meaningful. I thought that a hug would be a way to truly illustrate my desire for reconciliation since I knew that a hug just has that meaningful healing quality. But the young lady vehemently refused the hug and in a flagrantly sarcastic tone told me to "have a good night" her true colors slowly emerging.

I took a brief pause and replied very confidently, almost prophetically as if the words were mystically flocking to my tongue, "Oh I'm going to have a good night, but you're going to have a bad night!" and instantly she vanished.

Ten minutes later, John and I, bored and boozeless, left the party and *peace rolled* home. The image that we saw on our way there came as little surprise, to me at least.

I had faith that a strange presence was working through me all day. I was very, very religious in my youth, but as I got older and developed a sense of humor, my religiosity gradually faded. However, deep down, I don't think the true soul God gave me ever left. Now, since I was sobering up and coming into manhood, that soul just woke up from a long slumber.

So I was I was far from surprised to see the girl in the back of a police car after the soul-inspired warning. The young lady should have followed the holy call to reconcile. Instead she decided to drive drunk and get arrested. Hopefully however, we both learned from the experience.

John was amazed. If he was once skeptical of the legitimacy of the Revelation I spoke of, he was now a believer.

To ensure a sense of closure, John, an always-savvy film student, pulled his Honda Accord over to the side of the street, strides behind the BCPD criminal cruiser.

"Dude, walk over to her and make that straighten up symbol that she was flashing you earlier. That'll be a perfect ending." John instructed me authoritatively.

On John's orders, I walked up to the police car, looked the young woman blinded by a materialistic culture in the eyes and quietly made the "Straighten Up" hand symbol that she had flashed me earlier. In this brief instant I held, as if it were a miracle, a clear vision of justice. Then I forgave the girl and prayed that she would indeed straighten up.

After this influential moment passed, I felt a metaphysical calm pass over me like my biblical day was done. Because I felt like it was, I now sought a peaceful ending to my three-day spell of sleeplessness.

As I walked out to the beach alone upon my return to 39th, John asked the natural question, "Where you going, Castile?"

"To be free," was all I said. I had always flirted with the idea I was about to act on but never dared trying it—until now.

Running through the sands, I stripped down to my natural self and swam out into the cool but soothing waters characteristic of a July night in the Mid-Atlantic. Dancing in the sands, bathing into the moonlight, I felt truly free for the 1st time in my life.

Even though I was breaking the local law, I believed that I was following higher law by allowing myself to be free for once and swim naked.

"Dude, you guys know where Castile went?" Mark asked as he peaked into Chris's room.

"Said he was going to be free. Last time I saw him he was walking toward the ocean." John replied.

"Awww, well I hope he becomes free out there." Mary responded.

"Yeah, I have a feeling he will. Salvation lies on the shore." John added.

Following the period of moonlight bathing, which could have easily been two minutes, even though it felt unbound my time, I got dressed and walked, rolling with relief, forty yards back into my apartment. Upon my soaking but smiling arrival, a circle of friends greeted me.

"Castile, did you go swimming?" Mark inquired.

I nodded.

"Naked?" John asked.

"Yep" I replied.

"I always wanted to do that." John said back.

"I am *proud* of you, Chris." Mary told me.

"Thanks. I'm going to bed now. I'm pretty tired." I said to all.

"Good Night, Chris." Mary responded.

"Good night, Chris" were the last and only words I heard before I passed out, sprawled with a smile, forty seconds later. Deep sleeping for the first time in recent memory, I quickly eased into some timely California dreaming after a long, long, day of heady Puritan labor.

Flight

"People who do not break things first will never learn to create anything"
—Philipino Proverb

After some California dreaming, I woke with visions of sands and tasty waves dancing in my head. I was living in Beach City, Maryland for the second summer in a row with my best friends in the world. Unfortunately, I forgot this at times. Philosophy was my major at Sacred Heart and the human condition often felt too perplexing not to start examining. Today however, I was working on a deep sleep. Therefore the ocean and the sands, rather than the perennial problems of philosophy were at my core of awareness.

As I was about to stroll out my room, I heard my name mentioned and naturally listened in on the conversation.

"Dude, what was up with Castile last night?" Peter inquired.

"I don't know last night was weird." John answered. "He was saying all this stuff about nirvana and enlightenment and I didn't believe him at first. You know, it's Castile. He's a goofball. But that prediction he made about that girl that he thought was sinning was too strange not to believe him. He said it so confidently, like there was no doubt in his mind that he would have a good night and she would have a bad night. He's really smart too. And she did get arrested. He ended up swimming naked, saying he wanted to be free, and the last thing he heard before bed was Mary telling him goodnight. Mary's hot dude and really nice. And when I went into the room, Castile had this huge grin on his face as he slept." John followed.

"Yeah, I mean I think he just had a bible experience yesterday. I believe in miracles. I believe in Jesus. And I believe my best friend when he tells me something." Mark added.

"Maybe. Let's go to the beach." Peter suggested.

"I'll wake up Castile." Mark replied. I jumped back in bed and pretended I had been sleeping.

"Castile, you wanna go to the beach dude?" Mark asked.

"Um, I'm still kind of tired. I'll be out there in like an hour." I answered.

"Alright, we'll be out there." Mark replied.

Faithful to my word, I walked downstairs and toward the beach about an hour later. Mary was downstairs with some smiling young faces.

"Chris, hey! I want you meet some of my friends. These are Christian missionaries—Sara, Brittany, and Courtney. They're with Young Life. I was going to do Young Life with them this summer, but decided to live here instead," she informed me.

"Oh, that's cool. Nice to meet you girls." I responded.

"I told them about the revelation you had last night about forgiveness." Mary told me.

"Oh, man." I replied a little embarrassed.

"Don't be embarrassed Chris. I believed your story all along. It *is* very important to forgive people like God forgives us." Mary answered.

"Well, we still get two kegs of beer every night." I followed shortly thereafter.

"Yes you do. I think you're slowly corrupting my friends and me." Mary added with a smile.

"Kegs?" Brittany asked.

"Of alcohol?" Sara inquired.

"Yeah" Mary and I both said.

"Well you're lucky Jesus died for your sins." Courtney replied.

"Ok then. I guess I am. I'm going to the beach. See you later Mary. Nice meeting you missionaries." I responded just before I walked the forty-yard walk to the dunes and saw my roommates talking.

"What are you guys talking about?" I asked innocently.

"Something you wouldn't know much about Castile...pussy." Jack said in a polluted tone.

"Ohhhhhhhh!" was the consensual reaction.

"Dude, I fucked the shit out of Jenny last night. I was high as shit. You know how crazy you get when you're high? That was like me fucking Jenny. It was like I was in another world." Jack informed the group.

"I got some poonanny last night too." Mark responded.

"Me too. I've been getting like crazy boy band ass this summer." Peter said.

"These girls man, what a joke. They're easily just as horny as guys. All of them." Mark chimed in.

"That's something Castile wouldn't know. He's too nice to girls to fuck them. Seriously dude, when you gonna stop being such a prude and start fucking?" Jack asked me.

"I just think sex is something that should be saved for people in love. Sex is about more than physical pleasure. Sex is an expression of a holistic love two people have for each other. Without love, sex loses its meaning. Or at least that's what my favorite philosophy professor told me. So when I'm in love I will "start fucking" I guess." I answered.

"Pussy" Jack responded.

"Cool dude" I responded, completely immune to his instigation. I didn't know why he felt the need to taunt me, but I'd come to expect that kind of behavior from Jack Lewis. He was hot and cold all summer. Sometimes he was my best friend, other times he was my worse enemy. Yesterday he was a believer of my story while today he was a taunting asshole. I think he was upset about his parents recently getting divorced and showed it more times than others depending on how much he was drinking or how much he really thought about it. I couldn't imagine what it would be like to have divorced parents so I couldn't really judge Jack. Still, I didn't know why he had to pick on me.

Unable to make a valuable contribution while my friends, as they called it, "talked pussy" I declared that I was going swimming and sprinted alone through the sands and into the shallow ocean water.

"That kid needs to get laid dude." Jack's roommate Scott said with confidence.

"Yeah but Chris has always been so bad with girls that it'll be really hard for him to pull it off." Peter followed.

"Yeah remember what happened with Elizabeth Grey?" Mark asked. Everyone laughed.

"Chris is really smart though. He's a good kid and funny as shit too. He'll find a girl one day." John answered with prophetic vision.

* * *

Later, when it was dark out, I went back into the shallow ocean water for a ritual swim. The next night, I participated in the ritual once again but did so awake from the day before—but did so feeling like I had during my initial spell of insomnia.

I just had so many questions, so many thoughts, but too little answers or comfortable resolutions. Whenever I neared the forty hours of sleep deprivation mark during this rave, the red sirens started to go off.

As I swam in the ocean waters on the second consecutive sleepless night, I couldn't stop thinking about God. I couldn't stop thinking about Jesus. And I couldn't stop thinking about the mysteries that linked the two together in history and faith. On this night, I was unwell because I had been up all night for consecutive nights. On this night, I was launched on an astronomical thought-flight for reasons I couldn't rationalize without faith.

I got some sleep that night, but not much. And when I woke I felt like I was rolling on ecstasy. Something was happening to me that I couldn't completely control. I just didn't know at the time that it was fiercely maturing bipolar mania.

I sprinted out to John's car wearing my Eckhart Soccer jersey, #3, a sign of the Trinity, when I woke.

"Castile dude, what took you so long?" Mark asked.

"I had to find my shirt. It's a great shirt. An awesome shirt. #3. Just like the trinity." I responded like my mouth was a verbal machine gun.

"Ok, whatever Father Castile." John said sarcastically.

"Let's listen to some Crows." Mark suggested and proceeded to put on their sophomore hit "Recovering the Satellites". As soon as he did it, I refused to quit interpreting it, citing ethical necessity.

The coded lyrics finally made perfect sense to me because my brain was now bubbling with big poetic discoveries. Therefore, despite the frequent requests of John and Mark, my mouth rapidly relayed impulsive interpretations for the entire trip to Merryweather Post Pavilion—the site of the Counting Crows show that we were traveling to on this steamy July day.

When the song "Angels of the Silences" thundered from John's speakers, I asked him and Mark if they thought that Counting Crows lead singer Adam Duritz "dreams of Michelangelo when he's lying in his bed" because he dreams of being divinely inspired.

John identified with the imagery. "Yeah like the Sistine Chapel painting where Adam and God touch fingertips," he responded.

"Yeah just like that. I'm starting to feel like Adam in that painting." I answered. "Since that Good Night/Bad Night I've felt a lot different. It's like I'm seeing the Truth or something."

In my creatively colored consciousness, I did feel inspired from above. Whether or not the feeling was ignited by real revelation, I couldn't be absolutely certain. My bias however, was that it was real revelation sparked by my sleepless condition because, as the aphorism goes, "You have to be a little cracked to see the light." Real or exaggerated though, I held sincerely a sense of heavenly calling.

When we finally reached the concert parking lot, this newly spawned spiritual sense loosened the tight grip that brain sense previously held over my decision making core. Quickly after we parked, I observed a group of kids my age being cited by the police for drinking alcohol.

The kids looked between 18-20 years old, therefore old enough to die in Iraq, go to jail, and get married; but too young to drink alcohol because of the Neo-Prohibitionist movement. Thus, what was currently presiding was *Injusticia*—a cancer that I needed to cure in my Quixote-inclined view.

Fueled in my fanatic ways by this sacred spirit of social justice, I took a bold stand and spoke my soul to the Howard County police while they were endowed deeply to their duty of enforcing the law. I deemed such behavior, however unusual, an exercise of free speech-my constitutional right, and therefore legally justifiable.

I approached the police with a giant grin on my face, blissful like Clay Aiken at the YMCA, and said chivalrously, "Leave my friends alone. Kids are just trying to have a good time," with a sun dried smile twice before I finally retreated at the urgent instruction of the police.

My friends looked at me in awe, my bold behavior sending electric shock waves throughout their unexpecting veins. They had been shouting, "No. Don't do it," ever since I approached the police.

My friends, like most normal people, wouldn't dare voluntarily contest socially sovereign authority but I was paranormal at this moment. I was in a religious ecstasy—a word transcendent Flight where the call of the Spirit superseded the rule of the Law.

Quickly after my authority ordered retreat, two cops emerged from writing their citations ravenous for what they perceived as Justice. A shorter, but equally furious and imposing Reginald VelJohnsonesque (Family Matters Star, "Carl Winslow") cop said decisively, "Now we gonna deal with you," as he pointed his pudgy chocolate finger in my face.

All I was able to mutter was "no, no" unable to grasp the injustice of the situation as it was not congruent with my understanding of the nature of criminalization warranting behavior—my actions weren't harmful nor malicious therefore they weren't criminal in my mind. The other cop, a tall flat-topped bruiser, whispered softly in my uneasy ear, "What's your name buddy?" as he aggressively put his "hard working" hands on my sun burnt back.

Anthropomorphically tilted and consequently intensely aggravated, I got nasty. "I'm not fucking telling you." I shouted at the officer.

Almost instantly I was hip-tossed onto the harmless hood of John's car as I screamed, shocked and fear-frenzied, nothing but, "No. What are you doing to me?" just before I blacked out, seconds later, from the sudden shock of the scary sequence of events. In a span of less than a week I had gone from employed, even keeled, and peaceful to jobless, broken-down on a giant slab of concrete with police screaming ferociously at me. How fast times do change.

When I came to a clearer state of awareness, I quickly became cognizant of the hard fact that not only was my flushed face planted securely on the burning summer asphalt, but also that both my hands and feet were in criminal cuffs. Such an epic symphony of insanity surely would have made my parents proud as not only was I cuffed, face to the floor in a parking lot, I was also surrounded by a posse of police officers who all, like the Ancient Romans, barked the incessant order that I must identify myself.

The stunning scene essentially, was quite chaotic. In the heat of all the chaos and confusion however, I held Biblical courage and never abandoned my core convictions. When law enforcement informed me that I was now bound for the interrogation room, I quickly called upon this courage to save me in the current time of trouble and uncertainty. Hence, the ideally intense interrogation process evolved into a game of recess—for me at least.

I, on one end of the spectrum, was high off tie-dyed abstractions of the divine, yet still Biblically backed in my basic belief structure. The police on the other end were low on angry, black and white "this kid's a fuckin' asshole (rightfully inspired)" thoughts, backed by brutality. Because they were, a frenzy of outrageous interaction ensued.

Like a jovial jackass, I started making fun of the cops despite the fact that there were seven of them who all wore stone-cold serious looks on their furious faces.

"Did you have a childhood? I'm just messing around being a kid. I didn't do anything immoral so why all the violence, shackling, and questioning bullshit?" I asked the officers who were far from pleased at the inquiry.

"Identify yourself now!" The officers collectively demanded.

"Screw you, let me go!" I repeated numerous times, perpetuating the stagnant cycle.

Inevitably, one militant cop grew so frustrated by my stubborn refusal to identify myself that he snapped, reached into my pocket, and pulled out what he assumed to be a Fake ID.

"Look's like we can add a Fake ID to the charges," the officer said smugly, proud of his Ass-Clown of the Year Award contending accomplishment, content to criminalize my non-violent self. Unfortunately I had other plans.

A proud swindler of New Jersey ID's, I had devoted a disciple-like effort to mastering the art of falsifying identity during my freshman year of college. I did this primarily as, excuse the politically charged jargon, a youthful act of rebellion against an unjust government.

I harbored the strong conviction that a government whose top authorities possessed DUI's (Doosh Gayney, 2 Adam U. Rich, 1) were being so flagrantly hypocritical in forcing prohibition upon a group of citizens—18-20 year olds, that were old enough by law to go to war that I had to counter their unmerited efforts. That and I needed beer money. Therefore, I studied Fake ID law, downloaded DMV templates, memorized the doorman proof details, and set up a booming business in Paul Hall under the notoriously omniscient eye of legendary RA and fun policeman Big, Bad, Brandon Marshall, for the love of both justice and National Bohemian Beer.

In a relaxed, confident tone, I informed the cop that the alleged "Fake ID" was not in fact what he believed it to be. It was a "Novelty item".

"It's a novelty item, not a Fake ID. I never used it to identify myself and never will because I know that if I keep telling you it's a novelty item then you can't do shit." I asserted like the ass of a devoutly rotund, Polish-American I became when provoked.

The cop responded in a tricky tone by saying, "So you're telling me it's a Fake ID?" to which I shook my head and countered with the practiced statement.

"Nope I am actually telling you something totally different. Very different. It's a novelty item baby, not a Fake ID. I never used it to identify myself, didn't concede that it was a Fake ID, therefore it's not a Fake ID. It's a novelty item—and novelty items are not illegal in the great state of Maryland."

The novelty item defense was sound, shielding me from legal charges of possession of false identification—a $500-1500 fine in Maryland. I held a miniature sense of vindication in light of my slight victory, but I was still eager to see the Counting Crows and, at the present, chained and shackled in a police interrogation room.

Finally, my brain sense returned, at least momentarily. I disclosed my personal information so that the judicial process could progress. I revealed my name, parent's phone number, birth date, address, grandmother's number—all of that legal jazz just so I could hear the Counting Crows play music on this moist summer evening. Such was my initial intention. The officers, now sufficiently relieved, consequently recorded the information and hauled me—happy and tilted toward heaven, away to the local prison.

I use the words "happy and tilted toward heaven" to describe the moment because I was still in a state of bliss at this point and seeing the world with celestially tuned eyes as a result. Whether this state was the inevitable result of a careful cultivation of key "enlightened" teachings or just a byproduct of bad brain chemistry, I couldn't be positive. Regardless, I wore a sincere smile on my way to prison.

Sitting silently in the back of the police car with a joker's grin for about five minutes, I finally broke the sacred vow by asking the citizen on patrol, "Whose law did I break?"

I didn't think I broke the Law of Yahweh as handed to Moses. I knew my actions weren't immorally charged.

"The State of Maryland, it's my job to enforce it," the officer replied sternly.

My stomach immediately started to hurt at that moment and my conscience began to inject graceful guilt, because I sensed "intuitively" that I'd made a juvenile mistake by blocking his police work. Therefore, I offered an apology before explaining the logic behind my disorderly behavior as we worked, through carefully chosen words, toward a more sublime goal than crime and consequent punishment-*Reconciliation.*

I explained to Officer Berkeley—the tall flat-topped bruiser that hip-tossed me onto the hood of John's truck, that the Beach City Police department had made me frustrated with law enforcement.

"Officer, I've been living down the beach all summer and the Beach City cops are really frustrating me man. They're frustrating the hell out of me. They're drunk on power and get a sick high being dooshbags. It's sickening. So I guess I took out my frustration with those cops on you guys."

He told me that I wasn't mistaken in my general understanding of Beach City police saying, "Beach City police *are* dooshbags, man. They're sorry excuses for police and give us all a bad name. I lived down the beach for two summers' and they always tried to bust our ass just for fun. Listen, the only reason I busted those kids is because they had their alcohol out in the open. If they had it in cups, they would have been fine. But they were stupid and had it out in public. If the law is broken in front of me like it was then it's my duty to take action. I don't look for kids to bust like the Beach City PD does, but these kids made it so obvious that I had no choice as a man of honor to uphold my duty to enforce the law."

The nervous mood now stable, the young officer, reciprocating my gesture, explained the logic behind *his* behavior. "But we were extra violent on you, man. I'm sorry. A bunch of kids your age chucked rocks at our cars at the Jimmy Buffet concert last week. So when this know-it-all kid starts to tell us how to do our jobs, we're not going to take any of it." Officer Berkeley informed me.

The "aha" moment of insight now mutually achieved, the pieces of the puzzle forming a clear mosaic of justice, a real reconciliation became the inevitable result. Both of us former adversaries realized that we were both guilty, in our own ways, of making false stereotypes and underneath the criminal/cop skin, not so different after all.

"So now do you see how bad teens can give good teens a bad name just like bad police can give good police a bad name? I think that's the reason for the mess—we just misunderstood each other based on the stereotypes we both had." I told the young officer. Officer Berkeley nodded his crew cut head in agreement.

"Are you a religious man?" I followed in my Church voice after a careful pause, curious to see if perhaps the arresting officer believed that this reconciliatory experience happened for a reason.

"Yes I am," the officer said in stride with a proud nod before, inspired by the heightened moment, saying authoritatively, a few pregnant pauses later, "I'll talk to the Judge for you."

Lifted emotionally by his helpful gesture, I thanked my former counterpart earnestly before I revealed, golden smile on my sun baked face, that I too was a religious man. I wasn't religious in the historical sense where not drinking and not cursing makes someone religious but rather in the spiritual sense where truthfully seeking God in his/her own, special way, living for the affections—birth of a child, warmth of a good deed, and trying to practice the Golden Rule makes a person religious. And that's what I had been growing to realize in my recent series of sleepless nights.

"Ok, that's commendable. I respect that." Officer Berkeley quickly replied as a quiet calm soon set in. I stared outside my foggy window and locked my unlawful eyes on the pending prison—the inevitable host of my habitually defiant self.

"Loving your neighbor does no evil. It's fulfillment of the Law. The Word of the Lord. Loving your neighbor does no evil. It's fulfillment of the Law. The Word of the Lord." I incessantly said to myself, memories of a Catholic Mass now resurrected, as Officer Berkeley stopped at the district penitentiary and walked me, hands and legs shackled, to a session of finger printing, mug-shotting, and imprisonment.

"Dude what the fuck is Castile doing? Why is he acting like this?" Peter asked John, Jack, and Mark as they crushed Natty Lights in the concert parking lot.

"I don't know. Something weird is happening to him. Said he was being persecuted as they carried him away. I just hope he stops doing this shit." Mark replied.

"I don't know if he can help it." John said, and a careful pause set in.

"Sure he can," Jack protested. "Why can't he? Everybody can help what they do."

"I don't know, like why would anyone choose to act like this, you know?" John followed.

In prison I was not treated like the miniature martyr I considered myself to be. Condescending stares immediately followed my arrival in addition to a barrage of legal questions such as: "Do you hear voices? Do you do drugs? etc" to which I, a Suess-like criminal, provided the silliest answers.

"Well actually, I hear the voice of the Lord and he says "let his child go"' and "If loving one's neighbor is considered a drug, I'm high as shit right now." I responded to the standard interrogation.

One curious officer observant of my wild behavior asked Officer Berkeley, "Haha, You think he's on E?"—an inquiry to which Officer Berkeley quickly snapped back by saying "No man, he's a good kid."

True, I was in a state of ecstasy, but not because I was on drugs. Rather, I was up there because my serotonin (the "happy" brain chemical. Released naturally but also by cocaine, ecstasy and genetic predisposition to my condition) levels were running off the charts. Regardless of its falsehood though, the unanimous consensus amongst every Howard County Police officer besides the one who actually spent five minutes to talk frankly with me was "He's on drugs". I could see why they thought that.

Clouds

"To him that watches, everything is revealed"—Italian Proverb

An old professor of mine used to tell us that he had a great plan that would reform society. "Every one should get arrested at least once" he used to say, "and volunteer at a mental institution."

Now I can't say I've ever done the latter, but getting arrested made me appreciate his insight much more than my fellow classmates. Getting arrested for me truly was a humbling experience especially it was not necessarily a just one. Additionally, combined with my sublime mood it ironically gave me a freer lease on life.

So when I saw a group of teenagers about a football field outside the local prison, I trusted that they would be kind enough to give me a ride judging, in my post-arrest state of sublimity, merely by the fact that they were outside playing with a dog.

"Hey I just got arrested." I said to them. "It was some bullshit. Oh no, don't be scared. I just yelled at some cops. Do you think you could give me a ride to Merryweather?" I inquired.

They didn't agree at first. "Um, I don't know man. You just gotta outta jail." Dave told me.

"I know but I got arrested for being an idiot. I'm not a bad guy, just stupid. Listen, my friends are at this concert and I need a ride there. I am begging you, please give me a ride." I answered.

After a short interview, they understood my story better and finally sympathized with my situation. Because they did, Dave offered to drive me to Merryweather for $3 worth of gas money. I accepted the offer with haste although it ensured my current status as broke, phone less, and ticket less.

Ten minutes later, I was back in the familiar parking lot about to exit the car of a complete, but perfect stranger. Despite the pessimistic present though, I started to sprint ecstatically to the entrance gates upon my arrival at Merryweather. Fully confident that I'd be listening to the soothing sounds of the Counting Crows in the near future I playfully approached the ticket checkers and told them my improbable story after I said farewell to my new friend.

"Um I got arrested and my friends are inside. Here's my police report, I'll give you my gold chain in exchange for letting me. I interrupted these cops while they were writing citations but I am not going to get in trouble. I need to get in though." I said to the checkers.

After hearing my fantastic plea, the indifferent ticket checkers responded by saying, "Ummm. Ask our manager Bill, I guess."

Immediately, I issued an obedient "ok" but then just walked right past Bill, into the concert, thereby achieving the miracle of reaching Merryweather without adequate resources.

As an offspring of my current presence inside the classic concert venue, I was now poetically inclined to *believe*—not in the inerrant word of the Bible or the exclusive divinity of Jesus, just in the Greater Grace. I had ascended from the unlawful waters of police possession to the Promised Land of a live Counting Crows show. In the most Romantic sense, God's gifts of the trust, patience, and reconciliation were the wings.

Now inside the bucolic venue, I scouted the crowd in hope of finding my family of friends. Upon my careful search, young adults started to emerge from all directions, and greeted me with welcomes normally reserved for heroes.

"Oh my God, that was so awesome that you stood up for us. The Cops couldn't even finish writing their citations because of you. You're the man!" one of my fans exclaimed to me.

"Dude I can't believe you made it. I thought those cops were gonna put you in jail for life. They were so pissed dude. And that one guy slammed the shit out of you on to that car," one fan echoed.

"My faith carried me here." I replied instinctually.

Young people continued to slap my hand and cheer me as I walked in hope of reunion with the friends I had recently been shipped away from. Because they did, I began to catch a slight glimpse into the world of a hero, albeit unmeritoriously. I wasn't a real hero—I didn't risk my life. Not even close. Rather I was a young man with a plan to practice the Golden Rule who happened to get pinched while speaking in defense of underage drinkers.

Despite its lack of merit though, the experience of receiving heroic praise made me feel high. All I really wanted to do however was not to be complimented but instead to be in the familiar company of my friends.

"Help me find my friends," I told one of my fans who wanted to know if there was anything he could do to help me out. Of course he meant legally, but I had the legal side of my criminal case closed due to my reconciliation with the cop. Still, my peer was glad to let me use his cell phone. Eventually, I used that twenty-first century tool to notice John and my other roommates standing, Parliament Lights in hand, on the epicenter of the great hill.

When I reunited with my friends however, I was not treated like the tragic hero the other kids made of me. In fact, most of my friends were actually very upset to see me. I was in such a purple bliss from the praise that the other kids gave me and my tilted state of awareness, though, that not even the down, depressing looks of disappointment directed toward me could deviate me from.

Ignoring some of the ugly looks I saw, I invited everyone to read my police report because I believed it was a work of art. The piece was hilarious, empirical evidence of a kink in the political machine, but still backed in the sacrament of reconciliation. Some read it and laughed but not Mark. He quickly took me ten yards behind the circle of young life after I suggested he give my report a read and commanded me that I "can never do *that* again."

"Dude you cannot tell me what I can and can't do. You just don't know dude. You're not my mother. I'll do what my heart tells me for the rest of my life. For the rest of my life, Locke. If it means questioning alcohol citations, so it is," and then walked away from law bound Mark, returning to my family of friends while Bob Marley's "Stand up for your right" echoed in the background.

Shortly following my small fight with Mark, I invited Peter to read my police report but the skeptic, concerned with my curious condition, religiously refused. "Don't worry Peter. The cop and I talked—I'm not getting into trouble. We reconciled." I informed him.

But Peter, despite his ignorance of the case, boldly defied me. "Chris, you're going to get in trouble. I don't even know who you are any more." Peter told me.

I ended up not getting in trouble. But as for my identity being different, Peter did have a valid point. I was becoming more like a Suess character and less like an intelligent young adult.

Peter's words slightly pierced my Catholic conscience but I fought back saying intense and impulsively, "Fuck you Peter, I've got heart. You wish you had the balls to do something like I did and stand up against an injustice. I was given a heroic welcome when I got into this concert, were you? No you probably just stumbled in here like super cool, all-knowing, infallible Peter would. It takes real courage to speak your mind and nothing to simply stay silent."

"Chris if you keep acting like this I seriously don't want to be your friend anymore." Peter snapped back.

"Ok. Fine by me." I quickly replied and then walked over to where John was sitting, on the far left of the group, content to break off my friendship with Peter at this moment.

I greeted John, my always optimistic roommate, but then quickly sat on his left hand side and went silent. Scanning the crowd slowly, I noticed, sitting behind me with a sunlit smile, Noah Everheart. Our high school's most famous hippie, Noah, a Tolkien scholar, seemed almost monk like as he sat in lotus position, silently appreciating this sublime situation in tie-dyed attire.

"What's shakin', Chris?" Noah asked me.

"Um, chillin I guess. What have you been up to?" I responded, breaking my vow of silence.

"I just got back from studying Zen Buddhism in Thailand," he informed me.

"How was that?" I asked him in a rhetorical tone, sensing that it was something too great to be spoken.

"Amazing" Noah told me, but I knew that "amazing" still felt short of capturing the essence of weeks of mind expanding meditation in a Zen Monastery.

Seconds after Noah leaked the specifics of his summer vacation, the voice of Counting Crows lead singer Adam Duritz gently thundered throughout the crowd. Avid fans, we both turned completely silent, subbing out our Western voices for our Eastern ears. The masters were on stage.

After a few bars of evocative sound, I was able to identify the opening song, a very fitting one, "Have You Seen Me Lately?" and from that point there after I was married to the show. An unexplainably good vibration—a collectively high group spirit, gradually filled the 15,000 crowd starting with "Have You Seen Me Lately?" The Crows clearly fed on it as evident by their charismatic performance.

Lead singer Adam Duritz kept repeating the phrase, "This is our last *real* show in a while" from its early stages so I constantly speculated that the authenticity of the crowd, with their deep yearning for music that touches the true soul, gave it that real quality. But I didn't stop my deep seated reflections there.

I took a natural step in this soulful atmosphere and began to subject the deepest of seats, my own Romantic life—short-lived and uneventful, but in that short period extraordinarily powerful to critical examination, eventually easing into accurate reflections. Such reflections I have transcribed below.

The Dreaming Tree

All my life I developed heavy crushes on girls but was always too shy to tell them how I felt. My shyness and prude behavior was most likely a combination of the classic oldest child syndrome, my religious upbringing, and just a general fear of intimacy that I never really lost. Regardless, I had my first crush for four years and never said a single word to anybody about it.

Further crushes came and went, I played the role of the "nice, funny guy" all my teenage years and the more time I spent without a girlfriend or a first kiss the more intimidated I became to go after those luxuries. It was a natural but vicious cycle. But then this girl Elizabeth came along and everything changed.

Elizabeth Grey was the first girl to tell me that she had a crush on me *while* she had it. She and I talked on the phone for hours, laughing and flirting contagiously. Elizabeth came over my house when I was gone and looked at my baby pictures with my Mom. I never had a non-family member care about me that much before and honestly, I was at my all-time happiest during that brief period when I was with her, only very minimally for that reason. It's almost as if Elizabeth opened up a part of me that I didn't know was there—the side that Holden Caulfield never had opened for him. It was the Romantic side, the caring side, it was the side that means everything in the end. Historical tides tell us that it does very often take a girl to awaken this in a boy.

Despite talking for over a month however, we still hadn't shared our first kiss—I was a junior in high school and too intimated to make a move. I was worried that I would be a bad kisser because I had no experience doing it and everybody else did—much like sex in my later years, so I simply didn't try. But then she came over my house on Christmas night—the perfect time for a first kiss, a situation that was almost too poetic to be real.

When Elizabeth came to the green, wreath dressed door in a red Abercrombie sweater, wearing a fragrance that smelled sweeter then heaven, I started to go numb. Hands shaking, I gave her a Christmas gift, one that my mother had picked out, of an assortment of Christmas teddy bears. She gave me a hug, kissed me on the cheek, but I, too afraid for fireside Romance, put on Office Space.

I knew however that this was my shot—my first real chance to see how a beautiful girl's sweet, sugar lips tasted. So for the duration of Office

Space, my parents and brother away at the family Christmas party, Elizabeth and I snuggling on my red couch, my inner voice kept saying, "C'mon make a move."

I kept faking laughs until, inspired by the movies', "Who gives a shit. I don't care what other people think as long as I am happy" end theme, a pulse of Romantic energy surged through my veins and, in the heat of the moment, I looked over into Elizabeth's big blue eyes and said, "You know Elizabeth, this might be coming out of nowhere but, can I kiss you?"

"You're so proper," she said with a pearly white grin before gently putting her graceful hands on my red rosy cheeks, opening her moist mouth, and letting me lose my legs. We kissed like we were living the final scene of a Disney movie for a handful of minutes but then my allergies kicked in. God really did love me.

I started sneezing incessantly and went to the bathroom to blow my nose. Shaking my head, clearing my buggers, I heard the garage door open and felt a sharp sting in my kidneys as I was overcome by the cruel feeling that my special night was coming to an abrupt end. By the time I came out of the bathroom, my family was there to greet me.

The intimate moment now shattered "Meet the Parents" style Elizabeth decided to go home. Now bold and Romantically charged though, I stole a few more kisses out on the porch before telling her goodnight and watching her drive away in harmony with the angels. My first real kiss, despite being long over due, had truly awakened me to something special—something very special, that you can never know until you experience it.

A few winter nights later, Elizabeth and I were showing signs of being a legitimate couple. After we drove, holding hands, to my friend Anthony Triumphant's house in Kingstown for his little sisters' birthday party, Mr. Paul, Anthony's father, whispered some eternal wisdom into my unexpecting ear. A truly wise man, my good friend's father, and spiritually very aware, he whispered, "Don't lose her."

Deeply in love with his own wife, as my I overheard my mother saying about him shortly after he passed in 2003, Mr. Paul could sense that Elizabeth and I had great potential for God-given growth as a couple. I was too young to realize this biblical truth but did recognize that Elizabeth and I had great chemistry and cared for one another. She loved my sense of humor and every time I was with her I felt an added sense of being alive. Mr. Paul could see this in me when I was with her—he knew me since I was four. Unfortunately, my courtship with Elizabeth fell apart.

Blinded by alcohol and a sexually liberal culture, she did something very unwise and uncharacteristic, letting another guy fingerblast her and giving a different guy head on New Years while I was away on vacation in the Pocono's. My 16-year old heart as a result was shattered.

I heard about the sleazy story a couple of days after it happened and learned important details like it was at a party with " all older guys" and one that her own mother inevitably crashed and stripped her away from. I speculated that the whole thing was partially my fault, however, as my prudeness and her horny hormones combined with alcohol somehow contributed to this mess.

Regardless, blinded by teenage emotion and immaturity, I refused to talk to Elizabeth even though she was moving to California at the end of the year. I did this also in spite of the fact that she wrote me (what I now accept as) an honest letter in which she truly repented her actions. The guy she gave head to borderline raped her, pulling her head down hard while she was drunk and stumbling through a field, refusing to remit the pressure. The other guy though, she didn't write about in the letter and his Latin skin was most likely invited.

Despite this dim reality however, now older, wiser, and on the brink of an epiphany, I saw on this bright hill a better picture of what had happened: a growing 16 year old girl lets her passions get the best of her one night and her immature boyfriend vehemently refuses to forgive her afterwards. He does this despite the fact that not only was he instructed "don't lose her" by a beacon of wisdom. He does this despite the fact that she brought out the best in him. And he does this despite the fact that he was at his all-time happiest when he was with her.

So as the music spoke to my soul three years later, I realized three things, and three things only—that I still should have kept Elizabeth, forgave, and reconciled because, as Shakespeare so eloquently articulated, "to err is human, but to forgive is divine."

My Father always told me to be "the bigger man" and I knew had to stay faithful to his instruction. Forgiveness is a critical part of doing so. As the concert progressed, the necessity of this faithfulness became crystal clear.

* * *

The concert grew into one of the best I'd ever seen even though I had been to twelve Dave Matthews Band concerts but despite that fact, when I wasn't reaching epiphanies of Romantic revelation, I couldn't stop thinking about the bad blood that was brewing between Peter and I. Peter was one of my oldest friends—my friend since I moved to Bel Air in first grade and the tension between us truly tore apart my conscience. Peter obviously felt the same way because he wandered towards me, near the concert's end, to initiate the reconciliation process.

He gave me a man hug and said decisively, as if a product of long, careful thought, "we both want the same thing."

We wanted our friends to be happy, stay close, and celebrate life. We just had different styles of ensuring it. And that was the real truth.

So for the rest of the show, our petty differences reconciled, we stood side by side singing along to our favorite band. Truly it was a meaningful moment—a real reconciliation and therefore blessed with grace. But my battle-tested soul still hungered for something more than reconciliation with a dude. I wanted reconciliation with a former dream girl and something better than the loneliness and celibacy I'd grown accustomed to. I knew that something better was out there, I just had to find her. So, "I have to get Elizabeth back!" I shouted like a scientist following a breakthrough as I walked with high levels of joy to John's big green truck after the encore.

"She has a boyfriend," her friend Grace said to me on the way.

"I don't care," I responded with a Gatsby chuckle.

"Are you coming back to Bel Air with us, Chris?" Grace then asked me. Grace was a nursing student at the University of Maryland and one of my former editors, along with Elizabeth ironically, for our high school paper. "You might want to come home and spend some time with your parents."

Although I knew that going home would have been the healthier decision, as I needed to come down from the clouds with the help of my parents, I chose to return to Beach City because I felt too high to be around my folks. Furthermore, I believed that God had some Romance planned for me in Beach City—hence the Elizabeth epiphany. Therefore, my only choice was to return to the ocean.

"Sorry, Grace. I'm going back to the beach." I said to my former Features editor and then hopped into John's truck. As soon as I did, Mark was inside to greet me. He had a mandate for me to explain the rationale behind my disorderly behavior with the police.

"Chris, seriously what the fuck were you thinking?" Mark asked like a real hardass. Unfortunately he couldn't quite understand the explanation I gave him.

"I dunno, I just felt inspired to stand up for those kids. I did. I learned a lot. And they praised me for doing it," was my response.

When we were sixteen, Mark could understand my explanations, proclaiming, "I have seen the light and that is everybody sucks except for Chris," a couple contemplative hours after I told him why I didn't get involved with high school dramas. But he was a virgin then, an innocent boy, and in full appreciation of the fact that his best friend didn't conform to "cool crowd" perceptions of acceptable behavior and, by virtue of doing so, was cool in an ironic sense.

Now his mind was fully locked in the immortal task of "getting pussy"—reflective of my age group, but not of me. It's not to say that I wasn't after it, just in my present highly romantic state, the crude task of passionately pursuing random hook-ups was not the top priority. Seeking God, life's meaning and a soul mate were—hook ups were an added bonus.

Looking back, it's clear that Mark and I were on very different paths. Mine was generally spiritual, his was mostly sexual, and we couldn't relate to each other in our pursuits. I was in search of the trinity while he, like most kids our age, a threesome.

Preaching

"The worst behaved students turn out to be the most pious preachers"
—German Proverb

"Dude, Castile is out of control. First he quits his job, then he gets arrested, now he's trying to preach to all of us. That mother fucker needs to be put in his place." Jack asserted as he ripped another shot of whiskey from his 1st floor Pink Palace apartment.

"Relax, Jack. He might be onto something. Some of the shit he says sounds crazy, but other times it actually makes sense. I dunno, it's a crazy time to be alive right now. He might be a prophet in some weird way. Ha-he-ta-ha. Fill me up another shot." John responded.

"Yeah, but he was talking about his parents not caring about his arrest and he didn't even go home or tell them. Then he's preaching about honesty. He's a fuckin hypocrite. I'm gonna call him out." Jack asserted and then ripped another shot of whiskey.

In the lazy summer days to follow, I became inspired to speak about what my recent experience had taught me. The late night meditations. The sensation from seeing scripture in the morning light. The reconciliation with my arresting officer. The insights into the power of forgiveness—these experiences all gave me the faith to preach to my friends.

"You guys seriously. You have to practice the Golden Rule in everything you do. You have to love your neighbor as yourself. You have to because God wants us to do it and the world is falling apart. You can't trust the Church any more, people do whatever they want, but you still need moral fiber. So you have to get on the right path and practice the Golden Rule in everything." I told them.

My friends didn't want to hear any of that noise, but understandably so. Vaginal pursuits, keg stands, Ruit—they were the priorities. Not practicing reconciliation, forgiveness, and the Golden Rule.

In my more inspired moments, I would try to just preach simply their value and reiterate some basic universals as I thought the time was ripe for preaching the Good News. We were at a critical developmental period of our lives and falling addicts to many unhealthy habits.

My roommates and house guests boozed hard every single night no exceptions, ripped bong hits all day, consistently ordered Pizza Tugos—hot wings, cheese sticks, cold cuts, cheese steaks, and pepperoni pizza, engaged in constant, casual promiscuity often with total strangers and treated their bodies like dumpsters.

All my friends would say to me though was, "Castile, you've been awful preachy lately," and indirectly suggest that I shut my Gospel toting mouth. One hell-hot July night distaste for such behavior reached a peak moment.

I was preaching to a group of Atheists until I was violently interrupted by an angry Jack, a former admirer of my Genesis tale and fifteen shots of whiskey deep.

"Fuck you Chris," he snarled at me, "if you didn't care about your fucking parents and them knowing about your fucking arrest you would have went the fuck home."

Jack's charges were aggressive and unmerited, but most importantly, completely false. I wanted to stay down the beach for two main reasons.

Poetically, I wanted to stay at the beach because of my faith that being in the presence of my parents was not part of the master plan. Practically, I wanted to stay at the beach because of my belief that living with my friends in a beach resort beat living with my parents in a sleepy town in almost every way. Furthermore, I didn't care if my parents knew about my arrest because it wasn't the result of a downward tilted heart—it was an act of conscientious objection and concern for the rights of others. Therefore, it was an act that I was very proud of it for precisely those reasons.

But Jack wouldn't trust me when I said that I didn't care if my parents knew. It was unfortunate that he didn't remember how captivated he was by the Genesis story and how I always told him the truth. I thought such behavior merited trust—I guess not in this MTV generation.

As the anger in Jack's fiery eyes intensified, I decided to prove him completely wrong.

"Jack it's two in the morning." I said. "You're going to have to apologize to my parents for waking them up. This is messed up dude—it really is. But this is the only way to really prove you wrong so I am going to do it."

I pulled out my Nokia and impulsively dialed my parents. My mother answered the phone in one of those weak "hel-lo?" wake-up tones. I quickly informed her that I had been arrested on charges of disorderly conduct and obstructing justice—an ideal 2 a.m. greeting.

"Are you feeling alright?" She asked in a very worried tone.

"Um I am feeling alright I guess," I responded, "but I'd be a lot better when these charges are dropped. Trust me. I am not getting into trouble. I talked to the cop—I talked to him and said he'd talk to the Judge. He said I was a good kid. He said he knew I was. I am not getting into trouble I wanted you to know…"

"Chris, slow down. Why are you talking so fast?" My mother asked.

"I don't know. I have a lot to say. I'm not getting into trouble though but Mom, I gotta go. Good night. Sorry for waking you up. But please remember I am not getting into trouble," I said.

Then I looked over at Jack, gazed into his rabid eyes, and flicked him off. I tried to turn the other cheek most of the time, but the fighter in me emerged when Jack distrusted my genuine word without merit and provoked my impulsive self to call my parents at two in the morning.

As Jack tried to intimidate me with a Mike Tyson (late 80's) stare down, Peter brushed him aside. He gave me a merciful smile and told me to come with him "to talk". Peter was my friend since 1st grade. Therefore, he knew that something strange was happening to me.

All of a sudden I was speaking at a rapid pace, boldly challenging authority, and behaving like a preacher on drugs. However, he didn't know that the source of the new behavior was largely a biochemical brain imbalance and not an existential issue that could be resolved through therapeutic conversation. None of us knew this fact though and this left my condition a burning mystery for most of the summer.

When Peter walked me to the nearby street curb, my Godhead was still rolling with fantastic perceptions of reality. The ocean, the sand, the stars, the town—it all seemed surreal and my ideas seemed to flow like verses in a poem.

The first thing I said to Peter was, "Peter I've just been realizing a lot of things lately dude. It's like I am seeing the truth or something. Maybe God's working through me, I don't know. Anyway, I feel good. I feel great. It's like I am in heaven or something."

"Ok" he said. "But why can't you follow the rules?"

"Kids don't need rules. Let them play. Let them be free. They are just trying to have a good time. Their consciences will be their guide them so stopping forcing all of these bogus rules on them. Rules dampen the creative spirit man, so I try not to follow them accept the Golden one."

"Chris what you're telling me right now is just so far left. It's out there, as left as you can go." Peter replied.

"No shit it is man. But sometimes you have to be a little radical to see the right. And what I realize besides the Golden Rule stuff is I need a girl. I really need one dude. Elizabeth has been missing in my life for along time. She really has. Mr. Paul Triumphant, the wisest man I've ever met whispered in my ear "don't lose her" and now I can't ask him what I should do next. I think I want to get Elizabeth back but she's like 3,000 miles away. 3,000 miles." I said with layers of uncertainty. Peter listened intently and followed with some words of empathy.

"Chris what's your telling me about this girl Elizabeth, that's the same way I feel about Megan Blue." Then a pause. We were on the same wavelength, as astronomical as it was. Followed by a shocking revelation, "I wake up every morning to her face."

Not literally he meant, but with her picture in his mind. "I fucked up," he painfully remorsed.

"But Peter, you have Kelly now. I bet that feels pretty sweet. I bet it feels really sweet. Like what I had with Elizabeth on Christmas. I have to get her back." I told him before I paused and followed with, "Maybe the other girls were just teases of the real prize that make you savor what you have with Kelly."

"That's a bright way of looking at it." Peter reflected and our conversation concluded with a reconciliatory surge of optimism.

I walked back to the apartment complex and saw Mary cleaning up broken beer bottles outside her 1st floor suite, wearing her moonlit smile.

"Hey Chris!" She said merrily.

"Hey Mary!" I responded brightened.

"What's up?" Mary followed.

"Well, honestly…Do you want me to be honest with you?" I asked.

"Of course. Honesty is the best policy." Mary responded.

"Well, honestly I've been doing a lot of thinking lately. A lot of thinking. I feel like I'm starting to change a little bit. I dunno, I guess I have a lot of questions but too little answers." I answered.

"Well, I'm sure you'll find your answers if you work hard enough. That's always been my philosophy with school. And I know you're smart, so I have faith in you. What kinds of things have you been thinking about?" Mary asked.

"Well at first it was religion, God, and Jesus and whether Jesus is Lord and things like that. But recently it's been more about Romance and my ex-girlfriend and what could have been if a wasn't so shy and things of that sort." I followed.

"Oh, what was she like?" Mary inquired.

"Oh, she was really nice, funny, and cared about every body. She cared a lot about everybody. And was really nice and funny…"

We both took an awkward pause. There was a slow, deliberate moment in which a hint of the unspoken was mutually recognized.

"You know, you actually kind of remind me of her." I followed very carefully.

The awkward pause then continued. My heart started to beat like an African drum. The voice of Mary's roommate Kristi quickly ended the tongue-tied moment.

"Mary, come inside. I need to talk to you. It's really important." Kristi yelled out to Mary.

"Ok, Kristi. Be right there." Mary responded and gave me a glare that was hard for a novice like me to decipher.

"Um, Good night, Mary." I told my favorite neighbor and walked upstairs quickly.

"Um, Goodnight, Chris," Mary said back to me on my way up to the Palace 2nd floor and then went to talk to her best friend.

After my quick but timely talks, I ended up still struggling for sleep. I lied in my bed and as the sleeplessness continued, I started to daydream. The Sistine Chapel, the strange equations of love, Yin-Yangs, Jesus, the Buddha, and the recent best-seller—The Da Vinci Code, all spiraled through my tie-died mind as my roommates were busy snoozing, 20 beers deep. I stayed awake till about 6 a.m. like a Zen Buddhist on the brink of insight. When I did finally rest, and the meditation had concluded, however, I felt at a deep peace. It was of the only times during the rave that I felt this way. Perhaps the prayers for sleep had finally worked, if only for the moment.

Morning

"Great doubts, deep wisdom. Small doubts, little wisdom"—Chinese Proverb

My lucid dreams of Michelangelic inspiration eased into a smiling morning wake-up. The warm July sun radiated through my room creating the inevitable conclusion that today would become a golden stamp of summer on the shore—a beach day.

I woke up John and shared the good news. "It's a beach day, brotha. Grab your towel—we're going swimming." I informed my sleepy roommate.

With an aura of great expectation we walked past the graveyard of empty beer cans that graced our floor, down the sand scattered stairs, and forty yards east to the beach sands. As we settled on the scorching shores and set up our navy Samuel Adams chairs, we saw Noah staring in our direction, wide eyed and wearing his signature Bob Marley tie-dye.

"Rastaman's here." John announced. Noah was carrying his precious literary journal in his hippie hands like a security blanket.

"Let me see that," John said innocent of the journal's sentimental value as Noah wandered toward us.

"No" Noah instinctively snapped back as he joined our company, keeping the notebook locked in his kung-fu grip.

Judging by Noah's protective reaction, I concluded that the journal was his naked Self—a reflection of his authentic soulshine that he didn't want to expose to John in this lighter moment. Illuminating the journal's cover was a quote that Noah said was the bedrock of his thought.

"It will be a better world when someday the power of love will conquer the love of power"—Kate, socially labeled insane

Following a refreshing swim, Noah began to discuss his journal with us, thus giving birth to a morning discussion of metaphysics. Whenever Noah, an English and Philosophy double major at Mount St. Mary's University, was around his former high school classmates he couldn't help but initiate discussions that challenged conventional thinking. Although he didn't let us read his precious journal, his immediate insights did serve such a goal.

Noah's main argument was that people who stray from the societal norm that those in power would label "insane" often have the most profound of insights into our world to offer citing the "power of love" quotation and Jesus Christ.

"Jesus was wicked radical man." Noah said. "And he was crucified by those in power because he was radical. But would you not agree that his teachings were profound..."Perfect love casts out fear", "Teach a man to fish and he'll eat for a lifetime", "Love your neighbor as yourself." This is now the voice of truth but it was the voice of social radicalism at its time.

I agreed with Noah however, I pushed the argument in a slightly different but related direction.

"Yeah man. But the great irony is that his life and teachings have become so institutionalized that they've chained up the human spirit. It's either submit to Christ or go to hell. What about creativity? What about diversity? What about finding truth for yourself? What if I want to do something like do a good deed to commune with God rather than drink Christ's blood? I guess I am a sinner bound for hell then." I continued.

"That's why Sigmund Freud believed that "religion" itself was "Obsessional neurosis" or a form of madness. I understand where he's coming from, but I still think he's wrong. Religion is a product of faith, which is perfectly sane and natural to have as a person. The problem is there's a lot of brainwashing in religion and faith becomes perverted to having kids speaking in tongues in kindergarten. But try to witness a funeral of a loved one and not feel something unexplainable in your heart. Try to be human and hear "On Eagle's Wings" and not get goosebumps. Freud was just a militant atheist out of touch with the reality of God's Spirit. However, that crazy, German bastard was on to something in his critique of historical religion—the religion on church every Sunday or eternal damnation, salvation by the blood of Christ and the blood of Christ only."

"How so?" John inquired.

"Look at a Catholic Mass, look at a revival. Some crazy stuff is going down there. In the Catholic Mass, monotonous, dispassionate recitations, obsessive reference to Christ, and morbid mood. In a revival "Jesus! Jesus! Halleluiah", people speaking in tongues and stuff. All this Satan talk. However, these traditions are such a part of Western Civ that no one usually dares to ever question them. Freud did, and although I disagree with his view that religion is a form of madness, I do think there are some elements of Western religion that could be modified for the betterment of the mental health of the believers. Buddhists don't beat the psychosis of being in a sinner in their brains and the live very happy, meaningful lives. I don't know if I could say the same about most "Saved by the Blood" Christians—at least the one's that stress psychological submission to Christ and a life of guilt *over* following his universal ethic of unwavering love."

"Wow, that's pretty interesting, Chris. I didn't know you were that into philosophy." Noah said before he took a long pause and then applied his philosophical acid to Christianity.

Noah asserted that there were other mythological stories in the ancient world about a god who incarnated in man to save the world and the early Christians just borrowed that mythology.

"You guys ever heard of Methras?" Noah asked.

"No Noah." John and I replied.

"Well, according to the mythology of the time, he was born to a virgin, had twelve disciples, performed miracles, and died to redeem mankind...100 years before Jesus. How bout the Gnostic gospels?"

"No Noah," we replied once again.

"Well they were banned from the early biblical canons because they de-emphasized the exclusive divinity of Christ and the authority of the Church. Gnostic Gospels like Thomas, Philip, and Mary Magdalene saw all people as having the potential for divinity. Jesus was not a tortured savior but rather a wisdom teacher who had reached divinity and could help others do so to by feeding off his Word. So you can see why an authoritarian political organization like the early Church would ban these teachings and stigmatize them with the heresy label. Thank God these documents were discovered at Nag Hammadi in 1945 and are now treasured by many respected intellectuals."

I thought that Noah's newly revealed information was all very interesting, but dangerous at the same time because it defied the world's most powerful institution-The Catholic Church, whose nucleus was an exclusively divine Christ. To suggest that Christianity, as Noah did, may be a cult that borrowed mythologies of the day could cause chaos in Western civilization by undermining the authority of its most powerful institution. To suggest that Jesus was a wisdom teacher rather than God incarnate who died for your sins on the cross, could produce a similar a result. Regardless, it was a suggestion worthy of a Rodin-style contemplation.

Noah's skeptic wash of Christianity heavy on my mind, I proceeded to assert my views on the sacred subject of "salvation" in the metaphysical spirit of the moment.

"We should be saved in honest good works alone. Not necessarily the arbitrary will of God or committing to Christ, although that would help, but just being a good, genuine person. The world is confusing enough as it and there are so many conflicting messages by those in power. Sex is healthy says some doctors. Sex is sinful says some priestly figures. God is dead says some brilliant scientists. God is ultimately real says some genius philosophers. Jesus is your savior says some respected theologians. Jesus never existed says some renown historians. So what's morally wrong with simplifying Christianity in light of these valid conflicts—cutting out the fatty theology? Let's just say that Jesus was a great miracle, enlightened and inspired by a higher power to bring healing to a confused world and we can learn much boundless life-truth from his example. I just don't understand why I'm going to be damned eternally if I believe that? Because I don't believe I need to report my actions to a priest every time I think about a beautiful woman? And another thing. Why am I a sinner if I am a kind-hearted creation of a loving and merciful God? Because of a fall that was nothing more than the product of a Jewish storyteller's literary imagination? I am so tired of the so-called "religious" and their exclusivist dogmas. Practicing the Golden Rule should ultimately be the mark that makes one religious. Not whether they believe in virgin births, Adam and or Eve."

Noah and John agreed with my reactionary rant.

"Just let the Gospels speak for themselves," John raised Catholic said.

"My God is the God of Love," Noah raised Catholic said.

Both of these views could have been considered blasphemy, but the last person I knew who used the word blasphemy was a girl claiming to be a devout Catholic who gave Hand jobs on the first date, Blowjobs on the second, and Sex on the third, thus forming a Holy Trinity.

The most Catholic girl that I've ever met once gave Noah and Jack inept HJ's simultaneously! That kind of behavior is only reserved for porn stars. No wonder I was so thoroughly engaged in my search for Truth. People didn't practiced what they preached, seemed to crave sexual fulfillment above all else, and through my inquiry I had a sense that God was out there, but that the Times had him hiding from us.

Secrets

"Open Confession is good for the soul"—Scottish Proverb

The Pink Palace. 2nd Floor. Beach City, Maryland. 7.26.04

A lost, drunk, sympathy evoking Hispanic man showed up at the door to our house flashing his license. I could tell he was legitimately lost in a strange city and desperately needed to find his way home. So did Mary. We were the only ones.

My roommates all burst into laughter upon his arrival—pushing, pointing, and poking fun at him, not offering a single ounce of aid. Jack even tried to fight him. "Hahaha. Get out of here you piece of shit," he barked at the lost Mexican.

The scene was getting pretty pathetic until I, cognizant of Mary's overridden attempts to speak Spanish to this poor man, intervened and yelled decisively, "Everybody that can't speak Spanish get inside!" To my surprise, everyone eventually listened and the chivalrous rescue was initiated.

Mary and I alternated between grammatically correct questions and were able to determine the location of his hotel on 40th street.

"Donde esta tu sala?" I asked.

"Esta alli," he followed.

"Que numero?" Mary asked.

"Numero tres cientos trienta y tres," he answered.

We followed our questions by carrying his heavily intoxicated self one street north, up three floors of stairs and straight to his door, serenaded by drunken interludes of "ustedes son mis amigos."

Upon entering his tiny, yellow apartment, the Hispanic man tried to pull Mary inside with him in desperate, drunken predatory fashion. He grabbed Mary and started to pull her into his home before I intervened. A former rugby player, I authoritatively threw the man to the ground, looked into Mary's petrified ocean-blue eyes, and followed with a climatic "Buena noche!" to the floored drunkard. And in this chivalrous moment, I felt the beginning of a different level of connection to Mary Cooper. We had been friends all summer, but the chemistry changed slightly with this rescue mission.

Speaking Spanish together to save this man was very Romantic. Mary's care for him was very cute. My protection of Mary was very gentlemanly, and the whole experience brought us to a mutual level of respect for each other's sacred hearts.

When that drunk guy pulled her into his apartment, I was instantly overwhelmed with the instinct to save her. Instantly! No hesitation or second-guessing. When those graceful words of Good Samaritan Spanish flowed from her sweet, sugar lips, I thought, "Wow. There's just something special about this girl. Something very special." I had been leaning toward this idea all summer, but in this magic moment it came to fruition.

So there were definitely seeds of a newer connection sown that night. Whether these seeds were part of God's plan or just the random result of two people acting on instinct, I couldn't be positive. Regardless, this event launched the beginning of a significant change in the dynamic between Mary and I, especially because I had told her a few days before that she reminded me of Elizabeth. This was something that inclined her to wonder. For now though, the change was only in its infant stages and I knew she really liked Mark. So, I played Ruit in our house Ruit Room leaving Mary's compassionate company when we returned to the Palace.

Skillfully crushing the majority of our competition, Mark and I began to run our turf dressed table. I boasted an aged Baltimore Reverse-Hand throw while Mark, a classic but succinct Basketball stroke. Both were very accurate, especially Mark's. Through our practiced craft, we kept crushing our friends' dreams of Ruit table glory as we remained standing Stoically on the beach side of the table for an hour fifteen.

After finally getting bounced off of our turf dressed Ruit table, I walked outside, head-down, for some fresh summer air in hopes of natural solace. I was entertaining the idea of night-swimming as I walked disappointedly downstairs where, to my surprise, I saw Mary sitting still on her porch wearing the most confused of looks.

"What's the matter Mary?" I asked intimately, straying from former party-centric mood.

She looked into my curious brown eyes after a long pause and said, "I think it's funny how I remind you of that girl."

Although hard to fully capture in words, I sensed in this moment, that Mary didn't think it was a mere coincidence that she evoked the same feelings in me as Elizabeth—hence her usage of the word "funny". Not hahaha, clown funny, but funny in a mystery of life sense and that deep down she really wished that she could be my Rushmore. True of false, that was the sense I got.

Mary was very intoxicated so what she was saying most likely was honesty that she wouldn't reveal sober. She had been a Good Samaritan with me, witnessed my faith, and still my sights were set on another girl—Elizabeth. Blackout drunk, this really upset her and made her evoke the possibility in me that my sights should be set on her. I didn't understand girls very well, but again this was the interpretation I had to go with—one I had to put my faith in.

Her safety in mind first though, I responded by saying, "Mary you've had a lot to drink tonight. I'll bring you down some water," because she looked on the verge of a booting rally.

When I returned to her aid, pitcher of water in hand however, she had disappeared. I went to look for her and saw in a matter of seconds that she was inside her house vomiting. Kristi was there to take care of her and when I learned that Mary was in safe hands, my worry faded away.

Despite the inherent goodness I felt about Mary and I's tag team rescue mission however, I still couldn't sleep peacefully. All of the religious insights that had been recently brewing in my brain-Gnostic gospels, 2nd coming of Christ, Cult of Methras, Sigmund Freud, Salvation by the Blood, Golden Rule, Gandhi, Natural Mysticism, Salvation by Works, Revelation, Genesis, to name a few, mixed with the strange rules of attraction and my mysterious change in mind, fueled quite the heavy insomnia. I was still, God help me, a *virgin* and that truly made my interactions with the opposite sex very puzzling since most girls my age were not, despite being unmarried, virgins. Add that awkward sexual dimension to my spiraling psyche and you have a potent recipe for sleeplessness like the one I always hosted. Inevitably, although slightly drunk, I stayed awake until around 8 a.m. at which point I finally crashed, a sleep deprived soul searcher.

Later in the afternoon, around 3 p.m., I felt an overwhelming urge to get out of bed. I walked out of my bed influenced by the urge to see Mary, through my Pink Palace window, approaching our house with a book in her tiny hands. I walked outside modestly, directing my attention to the book she was holding—The Purpose Driven Life.

Quickly but nervously, I brought Mary off to the side of the deck and said, because I assumed she was blackouted the night before, "Mary, do you know what you told me last night?"

"No" Mary quickly responded, her tone fully engulfed in mystery.

"You said that you thought it was funny how you reminded me of that girl Elizabeth and you made it seem like you like me." I followed.

She didn't saying anything but gave a classic "oops" expression. Mary Cooper, on academic scholarship to Georgetown, had made the classic drunken slip—she said when she was drunk what she had been hiding sober.

"Let's go downstairs and talk about some things." I said spirited to ease the uncertain mood. Mary quickly agreed and we walked downstairs to into her house—unit 1A. To enhance the sickness (slang: coolness) of the atmosphere, I grabbed some Dave Matthews acoustic tunes, and used them as a springboard to one of my all-time favorite talks.

Quickly, as I was in a constant dream-like state and Mary, as she was in a perpetually happy mood, just lost our sense of time, emitting so much positive energy that our conversation bloomed into a state of euphoria. I laid on one couch, she on the other, and we gazed into each other's mystical eyes, locked our faces into huge smiles, and "dreamt out loud." Literally. We told each other our dreams and I felt like we were truly experiencing a piece of an Eastern reality. The discussion was so mind blowing, so different than anything I had ever experienced, that I went numb and froze on the couch like Sleeping Beauty (or more accurately sleeping Buddha).

We talked about destiny. "Do you think we met each other for a reason?" I asked Mary.

"I *do* think we met each other for a reason. But I don't like relationships." Mary answered. I knew why she didn't like relationships.

Earlier in the summer, I overheard Mary telling Jack's girlfriend Jenny in a very scarred tone, "Relationships always end in hurt," followed by, "I just got out of an emotionally abusive 21 month relationship."

So although I knew that a relationship with me would be much different than her previous relationship and most likely a very positive experience, as I was one of a select few of Romantics from my generation however, I simply respected her view and said, "I don't want a relationship. I just want to be your friend."

Mary smiled very warmly like a good guy friend was what she really wanted and said, "Well at this point in my life, I could really use a guy best friend."

DMB's "One Sweet World" now mellowing the air, we confessed enough to really go deep in our discussion. I finally felt relaxed enough to tell her about the Triumphant Family and how much they meant to me.

"Last year around this time, one of my best friend's dad died of cancer. I was really close to him and his family—they knew me since I was four. So I took it really hard when he died and felt a lot of sympathy for his family. I tried not to show it around my friends though. But deep down it really affected me. He was really religious and I wonder if he'd approve of the lifestyle I've been living. I don't think he would. I don't know, it's just a very confusing time to grow up. I can't imagine how his family feels. His son, my good friend Anthony, is not even allowed to leave the State of Virginia because he got caught without a little pot there a couple of months after losing his Father. It's just a sad situation. I don't really talk about it much, but I feel like you're someone I can talk about this stuff with. You know, you have a really big heart and are really genuine and sincere."

"I feel the same way about you Chris." Mary followed. "This book I am reading, The Purpose Driven Life…I feel like you don't even need to read it."

I'd never had a girl care about what I had to say enough to feel comfortable about revealing these sacred secrets to. Now I did. Therefore, as therapeutic talk poured from my vulnerable soul, I felt blessed.

"Well I want to make a positive difference in the world. Like Mr. Paul did, like my parents do, like my teachers have. So I guess that's the purpose driven life," I responded to Mary.

"I wanna make a positive difference too, Chris," she said back lying comfortably numb on her big, blue couch.

"I want to work in a children's hospital or go into medicine," Mary followed with a baptizing tear in her eye.

"I want to be a teacher." I replied, sun baked and smiling.

We inevitably shared our dreams—Mary dreamt of finding someone to "Dance around the world" with her to quote her favorite Dave Matthews song "I'll Back You Up"; I dreamt of being a speaker for my generation. We shared our ambitions—Mary wanted to go to med school; I wanted to get a doctorate. We shared our hopes—we both hoped to live happy, meaningful lives. We shared our worries—Mary was worried about leaving her friends behind and going away to college; I was worried about not being able to find work with a degree in philosophy. Therefore, my talk with Mary was one of the most interesting, deep, diverse, and important interactions I've ever had with another human being.

"We're oracles!" Mary announced with wonder near the end of our Open Confession, aware of the enlightened dimension of what was unfolding. Later she cooked me lunch, making me feel, for a moment, like a 1950's man.

Unfortunately like all good dreams, my time with Mary downstairs had to end—at least until the next day. Daylight faded, darkness started to spread through the Sky, and Mary drove home to spend time with her two favorite people—her parents. I could tell based on my long talk with Mary and her love of her parents that she really was a well-rooted girl—a well rooted girl that I was fortunate enough to openly confess to.

As a result of my relaxing day, I played Ruit all night feeling like a great albatross had been lifted off my neck. Finally, after a hard-hitting series of sleepless nights, I was somewhat soothed. The madness of my days of religious ecstasy seemed in the distant past and I had finally achieved balance in my life. All I really needed was a girl I could really talk to—a girl I trusted enough to share secrets with.

Following a few nights of regular sleep and big dreams I decided that it was finally time to return home. The power of ecstatic experience was apparently beyond me and I had planted the seeds of a fertile friendship with a great girl. Now, I could finally live the way I was intended to—with regular sleep, constant laughter, and trust in the natural way. Or so I thought.

Trust

"Never swap horses crossing a stream"—American Proverb

After reconciling with my frustrations of the Beach City life, I sensed sincerely that peaceful times were waiting for me in Bel Air. Through my morning metaphysical discussions, I felt I had made sufficient progress in my search for truth. Through Mary's open heart, I saw my opposite sex frustration dimming. And through my recent sleep, I heard the call back to normalcy. Unfortunately, my senses failed to foreshadow the way things really happened. As I later realized, there were also biochemical elements at work that I didn't account for. And those elements combined with a confusing environment brought me right back through the atmosphere time and time again until August and everything after.

On the three-hour drive home with my friend Julia and her family (my car stopped working again) however, I had no outbursts. In fact, I was able to actually impress Julia with my insights on the injustice of the current drinking age—a topic I had been very passionate about since my Fake ID operation earlier in the year.

"Julia, the drinking age is unfair because it puts a double standard on its 18-20 year old citizens." I said.

"Double standard?" Julia asked.

"The Drinking Age expects them to be mature enough to sign legally binding contracts, serve jail time, go to war, buy guns, and elect the president of the United States, but spineless enough to follow the law that says they can't drink until they turn an arbitrary 21."

"So how is it unjust?" Julia asked.

"America should not have double standards because double standards are inherently unjust and America prides itself on being inherently just. You know, land of the free with liberty and justice for all. I don't see how much freedom and liberty you're giving to nineteen year old when he returns from military service, wants a beer, and can't have one because he's not 21." I replied.

"Yeah, that makes sense, Chris." Julia responded.

However, as soon as my parents returned home and I was in the company of very close, biological family, my brain began to burst once again with an outlandish amount of scattered energy. Around Julia and her family, like I said, I was peaceful and well-spoken. But around my own parents I was in a frenzy of cacophony. There was probably some weird Freudian explanation for this being so but I wasn't aware of it.

I tried to tell my parents about all of strange experiences I had been going through in a very quick jumpy manner like I had been blowing coke.

"Mom, Dad, you should have seen me with those cops. You really should have. They tried to beat me up but I tricked them. I really tricked them. God helped me. I'm not going to get in trouble. The cop said he'll talk to the Judge for me. He was nice and we reconciled. So I am not going to get into any trouble. Don't worry…"

Quite simply I failed to behave with a hard, rational underpinning—the mark of an evolved human being. This failure worried my mother along with the rapid pace of my speech.

Looking in retrospect, it's clear that I shouldn't have filled her motherly mind with worries about my sleepless nights on the shore. The experiences—the good night/bad night prediction, reconciliation with the cop, Romantic revival, sacred secrets, to name a few were ineffable at heart. Therefore, when I tried to use language to translate them, I was greatly misunderstood and unsuccessful in my labor as a result.

I should have just my recent experiences in the Beyond Words, or as the Eastern mystics would call it the "True Tao" category and let them be. But, my impulsive, undisciplined mouth attempted to relay them anyway.

Consequently, I caused my parents to be seriously concerned about me and my current condition because, after all, a preacher on drugs doesn't make the ideal, obedient son.

When I read the worry in my parent's faces after I unwisely spoke of the Good Night/Bad Night prediction, I tried to save myself with some good, organic news.

"Um, well my mom. I gotta tell you about this new friend I made named Mary. She's really nice and we dreamt out loud at her house."

My mom laughed and asked, "You ever had sex?"

I responded with a shocking "No".

Then she asked, "Are you gay?"

I failed to see the humor in her comments and was slightly confused and offended. I was raised in the Catholic Church where premarital sex was a serious sin and then laughed at for not sinning in that regard.

If I was getting laid then "ha, ha, ha that's funny" might have been the appropriate response. But I wasn't and actually got very angry because of the joke for the messages that were being transmitted to me were in direct conflict. I was brought up in a religious institution that stressed abstinence until true love while my mom was ripping on me for being a nineteen year old virgin. No wonder I was so confused about the great puzzles of human attraction and intercourse.

Eventually though, the arguments subsided, at least temporarily. Darkness filled the sky and I rolled into bed comfortably listening to the Dave Matthews Band. Before I could snooze however, I tried desperately to clear all grand ideas that were weighing heavy on my mind but couldn't do it. I thought of Jesus and Buddha, Gandhi and Socrates, Taoism, Hinduism, Judaism, the mysteries of faith, and everything in between, including girls. In retrospect, this is probably why I had trouble understanding girls. Going from Christian mysteries of the incarnation, to Hindu theories of Brahman, to Eastern thoughts on estheticism, and then to girls makes for a very warped final mediation.

Regardless, Mary and Elizabeth were really starting to sculpt their ideal forms into my dreams. I guess the piercing arrow of cupid travels pretty fast. That may be true or, as I now diagnose it—a heavenly tilted worldview fueled by tie-dyed brain chemistry, a Biblical faith, and good timing creates very heavy crushes.

Regardless of the true catalyst though, these young ladies, through no intent of their own, were starting to soften me up. As I went back to Christmas with Elizabeth in my mind, I got chills down my spine. I realized that a girl actually cared about me enough to come over my house on Christmas Night. We kissed like we were in the final scene of a Disney movie and she wore a fragrance sweeter then heaven. How I wished I could get that sweetness back.

As I went to Beach City in my mind, I started to soak in the beauty of my God given friendship with Mary. Mary told me that I could be her guy best friend and that I didn't even need to read the Purpose Driven Life because I was already living it. She called me a "sweet, sweet man" and we spoke Spanish together to rescue a lost traveler. She believed that we met each other for a reason and said with humor that I was her "savior" because I saved her from a Mexican's horny hands.

Fully saturated in a spiritual sense of reality, Dave Matthews' ' #41 never sounded sweeter than when it permeated my room that starry night. The song just inspired so much hope for the future, which was a great thing, maybe even the greatest of things. And the lyric "I'm only this far and only tomorrow leads the way" was all I could think about laying at home in my big comfortable bed, light years away from the Pagan Palace that was Unit 3 of View Four Apartments.

* * *

When morning broke the next day, I woke up, as usual, with a sunlit smile. Upon my wake, I walked upstairs past my mom's Buddha statue, past the giant Christian crucifix that hung on my parent's bedroom wall, and into the computer room where I signed onto AOL.

Curious about Eastern philosophy and looking to make sense of my condition, I googled "Zen Buddhism"—a light hearted faith, free from prophetic scripture. In a few clicks of the mouse, I was able to discover a key fact about this offspring of Japanese Taoism and Indian Buddhism—that its goal is the deconstruction of traditional cognitive patterns for an empty mind and consequently heightened spiritual awareness. Locating this fact signaled an "aha" sensation in my head as according to my recent experience, I had scored such an unlikely goal.

I had become very spiritual since that Genesis-like day two weeks earlier and less traditional in my thought after the violent psychological shakedown at Merryweather. Thus, more empty minded and spirited, I discovered that I was close to "nirvana" in the Zen Buddhist sense. Nirvana is Sanskrit for nakedness.

Regardless of which descriptive context one could examine my condition from however, it remained extraordinarily powerful. To this day in fact, it has been the chief sculptor of my spiritually driven life. While the fact may seem shocking, my forty day rave has remained so.

Although it was very scary at times, I'm thankful I went to this rave. The psychological suffering—the wild mood swings, dangerously "high" states of mind, grandiose insights, rapid and scattered speech, that I went through solidified a strong character. The chemically elevated consciousness led to insights I never could have achieved through a healthy mindset. And, most importantly, the unremitting love that my family and friends held for me, despite my grandiosity, grounded my simple, but essential belief in the eternal powers of compassion and care.

As for the present though, I seemed, in the concerned eyes of the people who gave me life, like a looney tune—rightfully so. My first night home, I lied on the floor, psychoanalyzed my childhood, spewed out words like a verbal machine gun, and then stayed up all night in a purple bliss. However, I wasn't as worried about my state as I probably should have been. In my view, the angels were calling me—leading me into the clouds for a glimpse into the eyes of eternity. And their calls were loud and attractive. Therefore, not even the worried voices of my parents could keep me from hearing them.

During this Eastern educational inquiry, I noticed a Marcel Proust quotation that my mother had plastered on the wall of the computer room.

"The Voyage of Discovery does not consist in seeking new landscapes, but in having new eyes"

This was an aphorism that I could consciously identify with. I knew that my God-oriented experience and revival of Romantic mind had given me new eyes in which to filter reality. I also knew, in light of this fact, that my voyage of discovery was well underway in a Proustian sense not ceasing until my old eyes resurfaced, if ever.

In stride with this knowledge, my poetic understanding of this life-shaping summer shifted and I began to treat the time as a great adventure—a surf on the Great Wave of Destiny. I adopted the Protestant philosophy that everything major would happen for a reason known only by God.

As I understood my present situation in a poetic sense, using the wave metaphor, God—the 1st mover, initiated a wave and I was free to ride it if I chose. Where it would take me? I couldn't be absolutely certain. I just had to trust that I was riding a Great wave and I'd finally see the Truth when it crashed on the beach sands.

For the immediate present however, I was still surfing. Therefore, I had to exercise the virtue of patience on my board and joyfully inhale the fresh air of each living moment with trust in the Master Plan.

"Dude, Daniel. Your brother's been acting really weird lately. I'm kind of worried about him." Peter said just before he took a bong rip in the Pink Palace 2nd floor living room.

"What's wrong with him?" Daniel inquired.

"He's crazy." Jack interrupted. "Keeps talking about Jesus and Buddha and all of this shit. And he saying it fast as shit, getting arrested, and trying to preach all of it to us."

"I don't think he's crazy," Peter's girlfriend Kelly responded. "I think he just needs to calm down a lot. He's too smart to be just crazy."

"Yeah, but how do we get him to calm down? He doesn't want to listen to us." Mark input. A long pause of contemplation ensued.

"How bout' we get him a blowjob?" Peter suggested just before ripping the bong once again. Everyone laughed hysterically.

"No seriously, I think that's a good idea." John chimed in. "Imagine going through middle school, high school, and freshmen year of college without having a girl even touch your wiener, let alone blow on it and let it inside of her. I'd be crazy too. Freud said it

was all about sex. Brothaman' just needs to get laid and he'll be fine. He's been long overdue."

"Yeah, but who's going to give head to a goofy son of a bitch like Chris?" Jack asked.

"I think I know someone..." Peter responded devising a master plan in his empirical mind.

Buddha

"Good to sell honor for risk–Arabian Proverb

In a tie-died mood—the mood that my high serotonin levels paired with retreat from MTV reality created, I *rolled* to Churchville to play mini-golf with some old friends. Good friends since high school, we felt fortunate to be able to putt golf balls with each other in nostalgic fashion. Naturally, like every set of reunited high school friends, we shared old war stories about the glory days.

"Yo, Castile. Remember when you cut your hair into a mullet and went to school? Dean Parcy wigged out dude. That shit was hilarious." AC said to me.

"Yeah that was funny—it was really funny. But not nearly as funny as when Alissa Spinoza jerked off two guys in the woods simultaneously. She was student chair of campus ministry! And I am pretty sure she was in Young Life." I replied.

"Alissa Spinoza was hilarious. I could talk about her all day." Zach belched as we all nodded in agreement.

"But don't," chimed Lisa. "You guys are being mean."

"No that's pay back for all of those Jesus speeches she gave us." AC protested.

"Let's just play golf." Jesse requested.

"Whatever, go give Lou Testervault road dome." Zach responded to Jesse.

"You guys never change." Jesse replied.

As soon as our match began, artistically inclined as I now was, I started to romanticize my surroundings. This was a theme constant throughout the rocket summer. I wasn't seeing the present at concrete, objective value. Therefore it wouldn't be completely accurate to say that I was playing miniature golf at this moment. It would be more accurate to say that I was soaking in the majesty of a midsummer night in my hometown—that I was treating the nostalgic present like it was both a Gift as well part of a rising metaphoric wave. Accordingly, I didn't concentrate on my golf game and nailed a bogey on 18 to finish dead last. A fierce competitor all my life, I couldn't have cared less at the moment however.

I was winning in the game of life due to my recent growth in spirit. I also knew that being with my friends was more important than losing in some meaningless game of putt-putt. This was something I never would have realized if I'd never shed my ultra-competitive, "Winning in sports is everything," socially constructed skin. Furthermore, my unfortunate finish on 18 signaled that it is now time to *peace* to Alissa Spinoza's house for an underage keg party.

The mini golf game complete Zach, AC, Kelly (Kopowski, not Peter's girlfriend), Lisa, Jesse and I all huddled in Lisa's car. Zach put on Tone Loc's "Wild Thing" and made the familiar drive to Alissa's house.

Alissa had earned celebrity status in high school because her parents loved to travel and leave their daughter behind. Naturally, her house grew to become a primary host to the wild orgy of teenage rebellion—drug abuse (alcohol included), casual sex, and gluttony, so characteristic of modern upper middle class America.

As we rolled to Alissa's, I introduced my friends to a book idea I had conceived in one of my sleepless nights.

"You guys, I'm writing a book." I told the party of five. "It's going to be called, Everybody Farts, Hardass and is going to be a comedic assessment of the Hardass, you know like the football players who listened to Metallica and tried to intimidate the soccer players who listened to DMB."

"That's a good idea, Chris. You're a sick writer." Zach replied and then I stayed silent about the book for the duration of the ride. The book was merely in its infant stages and like Zoolander's "Magnum" I shouldn't even have been talking about it.

When I walked with a new sense of wonder into Alissa's legendary home, I was instantly enlivened. A soothing aroma of "sticky icky" (that special green psychoactive) permeated the party atmosphere. When they saw my philosophical presence, the hippies outside invited me to crash the session to contemplate the great mystery. "C'mon Castile we're talking about the existence of God. Come outside." Noah urged me.

Although hesitant at first, I eventually gave into the temptation to talk metaphysics in the green light. Perhaps these hippies could have benefited from hearing my apologist position.

As I sat down, I heard an ugly but all too similar tune—the tune of a Rabid Atheist trying to vehemently deny the existence of a power beyond the human race.

"God is nothing more than a simple delusion. God is a creation of our minds and doesn't exist in reality. I'd like to believe in God, but I can't believe in fairly tales." Christina Sartre protested.

Quickly after ripping the bowl, I ripped on her rabid atheism in light of my belief in God. "We live in such a mysterious, infinitely vast and complex universe. But there seems to be fundamental laws that govern it. I believe the creator and upholder of these is God—the Eternal Lawmaker or, as the Ancient Greeks understood it, The Logos."

"What laws?" Christina implored.

"How about physics? Love your neighbor as yourself seems to lead to an upward experience of life. How bout gravity? The law of conscience keeps humans from completely annihilating each other and the world orderly. How about thermodynamics? Good deed givers are warmed with great spiritual joy. How about homeostasis? The Love you take is often equal to the Love you make." I replied.

"Those are nothing more than culturally constructed mechanisms designed by humans to keep human societies orderly." Christina responded.

"Stop reading that scientific reductionist bullshit, Chrisitina. Do you know what that even means? You know how big this universe is? Wake up. Life's a lot more complex, a lot deeper than human science can account for." I snapped back.

"Grow up, Castile," she snorted back.

Then Christina cited Hollywood movie director/actor Gil Mipson as an example of "why religion is wrong." Her argument was a weak generalization that ignored the heart of what I had been trying to preach in light of my spiritual discoveries.

I was trying to preach the intelligent design to the universe as evidence of God's existence—not one famous Christian being a little looney. Still, immediately after Christina evoked Mipson, all of the drunk and high ex-Catholics began to laugh. Skeptical from lack of properly guided flights of thought, my former classmates laughed as if they were justified in abandoning their faith simply because Mipson was Catholic.

I mentioned my belief that Gil's mind was chained by antiquated, exclusivist, Pre-Vatican II, Catholic Dogma, noting that his comment to Warbara Waltwers, "I love my wife, but she's going to hell because she's Episcopalian," for the worse. However, I did add my belief that Mipson was sincere in his faith.

"At least the man has a genuine faith and acts on it. You know, Passion of the Christ did inspire ten's of millions of people. And none of us can claim to have all of the answers to life. He's a little brainwashed I think by hardcore Catholic dogma, but he's also a creative genius, you know. Not many of us can make movies. Mipson said that there's a fine line between madman and genius, and he walks it. I don't necessarily disagree although I do disagree with some of his views concerning religion."

"Yeah but faith is ridiculous. Science disproves religion." Christina objected.

"No way! It's ridiculous to say that faith is ridiculous. Faith is part of being human. Might as well say that loving your mother is ridiculous or showing emotion is ridiculous or sleeping is ridiculous. And science doesn't disprove religion—it just unveils the majesty, complexity and careful intelligence of a cosmic Creator."

The scene that we blackout stoners created was very comical. If any of the elders saw us eighteen and nineteen year olds, they would have laughed ecstatically. The depth of the discussion truly didn't coincide with the stupidity of our behavior. We discussed intensely the meaning of life at a party where the parents are gone. And we drank keg beer, smoked Vermont Hedis, and packed dips while we did. However, our behavior was justified—we were firmly rooted in the last stages of the "wonder years". During these times were our deepest searches yet also our longest keg stands. Rightfully so—we grew up in the most crazy, confusing, and uncertain of worlds. We were now young adults having grown up through the age of school shootings, terrorism, and widespread panic, yet couldn't even purchase alcohol legally!

My final words regarding the subject were, "The meaning of life is to live a life of meaning." Three minutes later, I passed out on the big, blue living room couch because I had earned it. Actually, I passed out because I drank nineteen beers. Regardless, I still had the courage to defend God although the traditionally religious would cast me a great sinner.

In the morning, I rose from the couch and my friend Steve Hullman drove me home. Bound to my big blue house, I collapsed on the couch for a seemingly endless period of time.

I was hung over as teenager on Senior Week. I failed to rise for hours until my younger brother, Daniel returned home from his vacation at my place on 39th street. Daniel's first words as he walked through the door were not "Hello. How's the family. Etc" but "Dad give me some money."

Daniel's words struck a nerve in my soul because they signaled backwards priorities. He hadn't seen his parents in days. Rather than greet them, however, he rushed into the house demanding money.

"Make your own god damn money before forgetting to greet your parents!" I snapped.

"What is your deal?" Daniel quickly responded. "I don't get you."

Daniel obviously didn't recognize the fact that I was concerned essentially with the well-being of his growth. But I accepted this fact. Not many people could see through my methodical actions, especially they were presented so bluntly and rude.

"Your friends all think you're crazy." Daniel added with a look on his face like it was something beyond reason. His comment made me so disappointed that it literally made me ill. It didn't reflect the voice of Truth although he assumed that it did. My only hope was that all of the madness that was brewing in Beach City would not be imported to my house.

In Beach City, my behavior was radically misunderstood, I was suffocated by sin, and every metaphor I used was unwisely taken literally. That's why I left the beach and hoped for exemption from it at home. It was obviously a hope shattered.

I invited my brother to my beach house, my friends mislead him into believing that I was "crazy" and he brought their misguided assessments back to my real home. Of course my friends didn't understand me. I was after the big questions, trying to get answers in order to lead a more meaningful life. They were after, to put it crudely but consequently realistically, the big set of tits, the "loose pussy", and the MTV-generated skuzzer who had them both. Their intention was solely to quench an instant animalistic desire. So it's not a surprise that they thought I was crazy—I was radically different, at least at this point in my life. I talked really fast about things people my age rarely spoke of and behaved very eccentrically.

However, I still had to trust myself and stay firm in my convictions however far from the cultural norms they really were. I was surfing the Great Wave and had to stay on my board—keeping my sincere faith was the only way. Even if that meant I was now referred to in private circles as "Buddha".

Patience

"Patience is the key to paradise"—Turkish Proverb

Thankfully, I was awarded a ride back to the beach with a person who not only sympathized with my search for meaning but also cheerfully helped me along the way. This person was Mrs. Sara Duffy, mother of my friend Zach and easily the wisest middle-aged woman I'd ever met. Inevitably she was able to guide me, through her wisdom, to a clearing outside the cave (to use Plato's classic allegory) that she had discovered long ago. But for now Mrs. Duffy just tickled my brain with hints that I was on the brink of something miraculous.

"So Chris, my son tells me you're thinking about writing a book." Mrs. Duffy informed me shortly after commencing our three hour drive to The Duffy Family Summer Home—a comfortable loft that rested quietly in Faith Beach, forty miles north of Beach City.

"Yes, Ma'am." I responded. "It's going to be called "Everybody Farts, Hardass" and basically it's going to be a call for people to stop taking themselves so seriously. I'm going to write about a lot of my experiences with Catholic School and underage drinking in it."

"It could be like a contemporary Catcher in the Rye." Mrs. Duffy replied before pausing in wisdom and issuing a comment that I couldn't fully grasp.

"I love palindromes. Words like dog and god."

Dog and God weren't technically palindromes, but I partially captured the basic concept—the concept of a flip, a 180. Slightly puzzled now though, I would experience the metaphor in its full meaning a week later.

As we finally neared Faith Beach, Mrs. Duffy asked me a relevant question but one nobody had asked me before.

"What's it like living in that ghetto, 39th street?" She inquired.

I quickly responded, "Lord of the Flies" recalling the Golding classic.

"You're right it is like Lord of the Flies," Mrs. Duffy said, impressed by the insight.

By the end of the summer this picture would be so clear that I felt like I was literally living a contemporary edition of the story.

Classic 20th century literature—Catcher in the Rye, Lord of the Flies, The Great Gatsby now flowing through our streams of thought, we eventually reached Faith Beach in concert with the fading daylight. Zach and I drank a few Budweiser's and then we were driven south to Beach City for the nightcap.

I'd like to advise the listener to please keep in mind that at this point in time, despite being in the presence of a Baltimore County Judge, I was still rolling. The insights were exploding like fireworks. However, the notion of the palindrome puzzled me. I mean, I knew I had been blooming, but how could Mrs. Duffy know that I was so close to full bloom? It was a mystery, but one that I trusted would be soon resolved. Mrs. Duffy had earned that trust. When my mother got hit by a drunk driver in 98', Mrs. Duffy, a lawyer then, handled her case and won our family the legal battle that ensued.

When I reached the Pink Palace, I wasn't greeted as warmly as I would have liked. Perhaps the kids had a lot more fun with out the Preacher Man around. Regardless, they were still hospitable. Peter invited me to play some Ruit with him upon my arrival and discuss this idea for a party that he was planning—a diaper party

"Dude, Castile. I got this idea for a party that I think you're really going to like. It's a diaper party," he told me.

"A diaper party?" I responded rhetorically just after I sank the back right cup.

"Yeah dude everyone at our house is gonna wear diapers. We're gonna invite all of those Hope High School girls over and they're supposed to be wearing diapers too." Peter said very enthusiastically while he took out the middle cup.

"When did you come up with this idea?" I asked Peter just before I took up the front cup.

"When you were back at home," he said, his shot rimming out as I got the instinctive sense that there was something more to this party than Peter had mentioned.

Very observant of people when they spoke to me, I suspected that the diaper party would more than a simple theme party judging by Peter's sly tone and the prospect of Hope High Girls in diapers. The diaper party would be my welcoming party to something whose welcome to I had long been overdue for—it would be my welcoming party to the pink side of the moon.

Peter knew that I was sick from years of teenage "play" depravation and, as a result, that sending a girl to "cure" me was in my best interest according to his medical opinion. Maybe sexual healing was in my best interest—the final cure for my sleeplessness and soul search, but perhaps my mind was still so fixated on heavenly planes like metaphysics and sacred mysteries that engaging earthly planes like stripping and spooning would be counter-productive. Regardless, if a timely hummer were the cure, I would accept it as providence. After all, it very well could have been the final stop in my voyage as simple as it sounded.

The Pink Palace. Beach City, MD. August 7, 2004. 11 Am

The morning of the diaper party eased into a beach day. Heavy rain was on the forecast but never fell, so Peter, Mark, and I eagerly walked the forty-yard walk to the beach. The previous night, after a strange session of green light reflecting and watching One Hour Photo, I had finally achieved my goal of getting Peter to ease his skepticism that I was going through a period of intense conversion.

As we blazed kind buds and tuned into the movie, I offered an interpretation of Robin Williams' character that when beyond the spectrum of any one's previous interpretation. Psychotic, insane, crazy—these were the standard interpretations of Sal. But I, carefully observant of the symbolic undertones of his character, offered a slightly different interpretation. I said the he "symbolized God" and was justified by his omniscience, his language at the story's artistic end, "who told you that you were naked" (Genesis), and his white, secret, presence in the final picture.

Peter slowly awakened to this conception and finally felt slight remorse for doubting that my eyes were receptive to "religious" vision. He told me later in life that he believed that I could indeed entertain wild but valid insights from my creative mind, at the cost however, to my overall health and organic functioning.

Peter's diagnosis most likely was in the most accordance with reality. Mark thought the interpretation was precise and accurate, the result of carefully piecing together a complex puzzle from an abstract angle.

So that morning on the beach sands, I took the next logical step and tried to convince my friends of two important, interrelated things—one, that I was truly going through a period of intense "religious" reformation. And two, that because I was doing so, that they should forgive my strange behavior since it was merely a steppingstone to new life.

Ultimately though, looking in retrospect from a more objective lens, the change wasn't simply "religious" reformation. The change was hyper-religiosity spawned by a serotonin spun "out of body" state that enabled heightened ability to insight at the cost of organic, healthy, societal functioning. Regardless, to supplement my selective words, I told the boys the story of Mr. Paul Triumphant—a religious hero of mine who I knew was a great man whether I was tilted or balanced.

Story of Paul Triumphant

During my junior year at Eckhart, I asked Mr. Paul what Moby Dick symbolized. Mr. Paul responded almost apologetically, "I said he symbolized God but that came at a point in my life when I was seeing God in everything."

After "Seeing God in everything" Mr. Paul became an incredible man of purpose driven action shaping his life after Jesus Christ. He wrote to lawmakers instituting tougher penalties for possessors of child pornography in Maryland and lived his calling by building Churches.

"Mr. Paul has been a real inspiration through these wonder years. He really has. If I never met him, I probably wouldn't be thinking about religion. But he was different than most really religious people. Really different. He was funny and he was faithful. It's like God told him a secret or something and that secret was funny yet still true and sacred at the same time."

The boys listened sympathetically but Peter was quick to point out some of the ridiculous things I had said during the grandiose state I'd been in for the last three weeks.

"You said the other day that you wanted to become mayor of Bel Air so that you could prevent it from modernization." Peter objected.

I countered, "Maybe I was just worried about my new hometown vanishing because I've never really had one." (My former hometown, a neighborhood in Baltimore City, had crumbed into a ghetto).

Peter deemed my response acceptable and after a few more Q and A's a sense of understanding swept through Peter's rational side. Even after our conversation reached complete understanding and true balance however, he assumed like I couldn't really see though his plan of a "Diaper Party". Peter didn't give my skill of careful observation enough credit as I didn't give his medical vision its rightful respect.

As 3 p.m. approached, I got a Wawa Roast Beef Sub hunger pang so I left the beach to peace roll to Wawa with Mark. Peter stayed on the beach talking.

"Ready for tonight?" Peter asked a tan young lady that approached him.

"Um yeah. I guess. I don't really want to do this but if you think it'll help him I will," she responded.

"Yeah, I mean he needs that help. He's never been able to work game and has always been too nice of a guy." Peter said back.

"Yeah I can tell," she replied.

"But now it's catching up to him. He's taken all of these philosophy classes and thinks he's Buddha or something. Little does he know that getting a blowjob is the real nirvana." Peter added.

"Awwww. Poor guy. It's so cute though the way he treats girls though. Like they're all angels," she said.

"Yeah, he's pretty naïve." Peter concluded.

After a nostalgic session of pick-up soccer at North Side Park, Peter, Mark, John, and I made the routine trip to Delaware to buy booze. We bought the two kegs as usual and returned home. When we reached the Palace, I rolled into my sand scattered room, hopped in the shower, put on my diaper, and immediately started to get low.

As our diaper party developed, I slowly began to sense that everybody else knew about Peter's charitable plan for me. Every one of my roommates kept flashing me ominous glances and John made me pay close attention to the lyrics of "Take me Home Tonight". I figured that Peter had told them to play along with the perfect plan and that they were very happy for me in light of the butt I might soon get. Who the missionary was though, I couldn't be certain. There were plenty of easy girls at the party but none of them had even flirted with me, probably out of habit.

In search of some summer air, about an hour into the diaper party, I walked out on my deck and joined twenty five or so party goers. Only three were wearing diapers. None of them were female. The more I slugged on my Natty Light keg beer, the more I thought that maybe the secret plan was only a product of my wild imagination.

When Mary pulled up to the Palace parking lot in her Green Volvo, I thought it would be relieving to talk to her about the situation. So upon Mary's arrival, I started to sift my way to the crowd until I saw Peter greet her. Then I froze. Peter looked into Mary's big, ocean-blue eyes, smiled, and said prophetically,

"It's Time"

"Ok, I'm ready," Mary responded.

"Where is he?" She followed.

"He's upstairs." Peter answered.

"No way. Mary is the one! Can't be true." I exclaimed silently.

"But why would Peter tell her it's time the way he did?" I pondered. "I sensed a plan all along and Peter's greeting of Mary verifies it. This all makes sense now. That's why everyone has been acting differently towards me since I got back. This is why no girl has flirted with me. Mary is the one."

From the time Mary walked meekly into our party minutes later however, there was an awkward vibe flowing between us. I now knew about Peter's plan and most likely sent off unconscious signals to indicate that I didn't appreciate our friendship being reduced to something as meaningless as this.

I think Mary felt this way too and deep down, didn't like the idea of being the missionary in some plan to get a sex deprived nineteen year old his first hummer. Especially one she had respect for. Instead, as Mark found out, she preferred to be the pawn in her own plan to hook-up with a tall, attractive frat boy.

I took a wizz around midnight and when I came out of the bathroom, I saw Mary tip toe into my bedroom with Mark. At this point I felt my heart shatter and my head get dizzy from the pure injustice of it all. I mean, I knew that Mary was attracted to Mark. I realized that she was a young, good-looking girl in a very horny generation. But this was my one special night, like a birthday party or something. Castile getting his first hummer makes for better poetry than Mark getting his hundredth.

Deep down, I didn't want the plan to go through, but on the surface I would have loved to get a charity hummer. So this human, sexual side thought, "Mark? Oh man! Am I really so pathetic that I can't even get charity head. This shit is unreal. Mark has plenty of hook-ups and on the one night I was supposed to have one, he has his hundredth. "

I thought I deserved to receive felatio at least once in my young life. Mark, along with everybody else in the house had experienced it more than plenty of times, but not I. I just got cock blocked in the middle of inheriting a biochemical brain imbalance never being formally introduced to sexual pleasure. Sickness was the inevitable result.

I went outside shattered and teary eyed, fixated on the *a posteriori*—based notion that I had awful luck with women. A posteriori is Latin for "in accordance with reality".

While I was in the process of shaking my head in disappointment, John came outside and said confidently, "You're shaking your head because of Mark and Mary," and instantly thereafter I nodded, broken in spirits.

John sensed the potential Romantic chemicals that could thrive between Mary and I. We were both nice, smart people with great parents.

We both believed in the sovereignty of the Golden Rule and cared about each other. We both loved to laugh and have fun, but also to help people and make a difference. And John, the movie mind could see this. So he said, "Mark and Mary is messed up. He doesn't appreciate her like you do. It's not right man. You deserve a hummer too," and I just nodded, a hopeless Romantic sulking on the porch.

In the beginning of the summer Mark, John, Peter, and I had talked about our hook-ups. Mark said he had too many to count—so did John and Peter. I only required one finger. So, "Why can't a get a girl?" I thought quietly. Moments later, however, I had the classic answer—"Only God knows why."

Amidst all of these potent feelings of confusion and anger towards the sexual injustices that reign disproportionately amongst my group of friends, a beacon of egg white light shined through that night in Beach City. The idea that maybe, however bizarre on the surface, this was all somehow part of God's master plan was born.

"Maybe the Mark and Mary hook-up is a lesson for me to learn. Getting head will lead me into a trap, driving me away from the spiritual one I am destined to chart and instead leading solely to carnal pursuits. Maybe it's my mission to be celibate during these years of sexual promiscuity so I can strengthen my character, truly appreciate my future wife, and gain wisdom by fixating my mind on higher, spiritual planes." I told myself.

Now optimistically genuflecting on the deck, I started to derive meaning from my lack of teenage "random play". I realized that the majority of males and females in my generation were consuming birds in Hindu language. They desired a lot of sexual fulfillment and got plenty, but were always looking for more and thus never satisfied. I, on the other hand, was in the most virtuous group of people as the Hindus saw it—I was an observing bird, a watcher insightfully commentating on the human condition. Currently, I was navigating a predestined path to Truth and rarely disappointed because I desired very little.

Only now did I realize that all of the blown opportunities to score led me to where I was today—on the brink of an epiphany, one of the deepest soul searchers of my MTV generation. As silly as it sounded, I was cock-blocked once again for a higher purpose. Or at least that's the mystical interpretation of me striking out once again.

As for the rest of the night, Jack had his diaper ripped off and had sex with Gina. Mark had his diaper ripped off by Mary but got merely a sweet HJ (as John witnessed while he accidentally opened the door to our room), Luke (One of Jack's roommates) was at Grace's having sex, Scott (One of Jack's roommates) was on 38th street having sex, Peter was having sex in the shower with Kelly, and I was in my bed with the light on meditating like a chaste monk. My faith in the virtue of patience allowed me to tolerate the rainy seasons of my life and gave me a sexual discipline much stronger than most.

As a testament to this faith was the fact that I was legitimately happy despite the fact that I had never received sexual pleasure in seven years of the era that experts call the "years of sexual discovery". Truly this was a manifestation of the amazing inner strength drawn from sources historically deemed "religious".

If I didn't have faith in a just God, then I would probably have been in a padded white room at this point, ineffably ill from beyond repair from celibacy and a furious sleep stealing condition. But I did have a sincere faith rooted in patiently waiting for God's plan to unfold. So when Mary came into my room late night, blew me a kiss, and said, "I'll *see* you tomorrow, Chris," very suggestive and seductively, I trusted that I'd inevitably reconcile with my sexual frustration and then be able to see the world without my virgin blinders.

My moment of physical transcendence could have easily been tomorrow, or it could have very well been ten years ahead, but I held genuine faith that my Time would come some day and then I would truly enter the Kingdom of Heaven as described in the Gospel of Thomas-

"When you make the two like the one, and when you make the inside like the outside and the outside like the inside, and the above like the below, and when you make the male and the female one and the same…then you will enter the kingdom of heaven."

Grace

"God loves each of us as if there were only one of us."
—Augustinian Proverb

Growing up, I had always heard stories about Born-Again Christians. Most of them were told in a sarcastic manner. "You hear about Mr. Walker? Went crazy. Said he found Jesus," or "You hear about Tim Rhodes? He's a born-again Christian now. Won't stop talkin' about Jesus. He's really weird," were the only examples of the manner in which "born-again" was used. But as I would come to find out, being born-again is not worthy of ridicule—it's worthy of praise and reverence because it's a miracle. I know this because by the end of the day I would be granted such a miracle.

I would not become a "born-again" Christian in the sense that most people understand it. I wouldn't tote around the King James Bible and talk about being saved by the blood of Christ. I would be born again without doubt. But born again in Spirit, in vision, like the speaker in Keats' "Ode to Psyche"—not in the Popular Protestant manner like Kirk Cameron. However, I never could have guessed that I would discover, on this routine August day, the meaning behind Judge Duffy's palindrome metaphor and therefore awaken from my dogmatic slumber. Today felt just like any ordinary day, for me at least.

When the damp morning broke, I was still pretty much awake from the night before with so many thoughts registering through my brain that sleep had barely been achieved. I rose from my 6—9 a.m. nap, as usual, cacophonous and cracked out. When I heard the good news, in the form of Mark yelling to me, "Castile! Roooooooooot! The Duffy House, baby. Today!" however, my condition quickly improved.

Last year's inaugural tournament had satisfied my healthy appetite for exciting Ruit, bordering on legendary status. Mark and I recorded fifteen straight victories including seven earlier in the night to capture the title. Not only were we strong players but we also had great chemistry. And that was the secret to our unstoppable play. But now our friendship was on a gradual decline.

My serotonin spun condition oftentimes brought out the worse in me and Mark was often the prime target of the ugly side of my speech during this anti-authoritarian rave. On the car ride to Faith Beach however, I tried to reconcile. Mark was my best friend and being on bad terms with him was starting to scratch my soul.

I told Mark that I had been acting different lately for one, because I had a crush on Mary and two, because I was "starting to see how God works" as I put it.

"I didn't know you liked Mary." Mark replied somewhat disappointed as he recalled the previous night's HJ. Fortunately though, Mark now understood, at least partially, the reason for the change and couldn't completely blame me for everything I did.

The mood significantly toned down, we began to reminisce about last year's tournament as well as other adventures from the halcyon days when my condition was mild and our friendship, as a consequence, was vibrant.

"Remember last year dude? We took down everybody. We stood on the table all night." Mark asked.

"Of course, I remember. We're sick Ruit partners." I responded.

By the time we reached the Duffy Family Summerhouse in all of its brilliance around mid-afternoon, in fact, Mark and I were laughing and reminiscing as if our friendship had never taken an unfortunate turn to Negative Town. We were now, after taking several healthy steps toward absolute reconciliation, primed to play quality Ruit. But the annual tournament would not commence for hours. And so, I just sat down on a chair outside the house and soaked the beauty of the town, the joy of the moment coloring my mind with an oceanic bliss.

When Judge Duffy returned home from the supermarket a handful of minutes later she quickly gave me an award-winning smile.

"You're like a boomerang!" She told me in a mystical pitch.

Then Judge Duffy put her crystal hands on my tie-dyed head and, like an oracle, whispered, "How does it feel?"

Quickly, I realized with clarity, that this woman was truly wise. This was clear through both intuitive sense and fact.

Deep down, I sensed she was enlightened—like she had a profound sense of life's meaning. Empirically, she was the only person that I encountered on my Surf that truly grasped how amazing I was feeling. Naturally I wondered whether she had some sort of psychic intuition or knew what I was very close to getting and how it felt to be on the brink of being "born-again" because of life experience. The latter interpretation, I believe, proved to be the truthful one.

My meditative moments eventually passed, darkness finally fell, and the August celebration consequently began in the yard.

"Play Ruit!" Zach announced just after the final Tiki torch was lit, thereby initiating the sloppy festivities.

Mark and I, the defending champs, easily won our early matches with precision shooting and streaky cup sinking. Mark was easily the best player in our circle of associates and I was a pretty consistent #2 man. Combined with a friendship now on the upward slope, we made solid teammates.

Our early matches now W's in the record books, the second round patiently waiting in the near future, I walked inside in search of a satisfying cup of cold water. It was inside this cozy south Delaware home that I saw Judge Duffy—the oracle, smiling ecstatically. She had a glass of red wine in her hand and an older woman resembling her likeness was by her side.

"Chris, this is my mother!" Judge Duffy told me as if she was in tune with the great mystery of my current state of life.

After her carefully chosen words, I felt an unbelievable surge of energy radiate throughout by body and was chilled by the ineffable intuition that I was soo, soo close to "getting it". Accordingly, I now felt on the brink of something miraculous and Beyond Words in this moment. It was almost I could sense, in a deeply metaphysical manner, the celestial love that flowed through the hearts of Judge Duffy and her mother, which allowed me to rise, rise to the pinnacles of Joy.

When I returned to the sticky, moonlit, Delaware sky, the miracle quickly came true. A familiar song echoed through the atmosphere—"Anna Begins" by the Counting Crows, and the "aha" moment, like a scientist's great discovery, went off like fireworks.

"Anna Begins. Oh my God, Anna's a palindrome. I got it! It's a New Beginning!" I shouted as I ran, danced, and screamed thrilled beyond limits.

My behavior became a spirited celebration of a great mystery unraveled in the white light. I sensed that I was finally experiencing what the Puritans called "re-generation" and what contemporaries call being "Born-Again." In light of this wonderful achievement—which has changed my life for the better on so many levels, I danced, ran, and screamed like I had looked into the eyes of eternity.

Love

"God is love, and he who abides in love, abides in God, and God in him"
—Johnian Proverb

Ever since the incredible instant when I discovered the hidden meaning behind Judge Duffy's palindrome puzzle, I felt born-again. I felt with faith that God had indeed cleansed my heart and put a new and right spirit within me because I've never felt the same since. I've retained my sense of humor but never again will I doubt the reality of God's presence and grace. Never again will I live without purpose.

Without Judge Duffy's wisdom however, I'm not sure that I could have scored such a meaningful goal at this young age. Her role in my path to Truth was so instrumental that I couldn't take sole credit for it—The Grace of God, the love of my family and friends, and of course her timely wisdom were all key players. Despite this miracle, which I pictured as simply a mental state of clarity or, to use Plato's classic allegory—a clearing outside the cave, I wasn't certain the wave had crashed. The summer was still breathing life and I wasn't yet ready to accept my journey as completed for I still had many questions.

So when we drove back to the beach sands, forty minutes after Mark and I successfully defended our title, the search labored on. I unwisely spoke of being born-again by saying, "Dude, it's like I'm seeing the truth or something." Then John stopped me.

"Castile, ok. We've been talking a lot lately." He said. "And when you say things, they may make sense to you, but when you say them out loud, they don't make sense to us and sound crazy."

"Nobody understands me." I replied disappointedly.

Kevin Anselm, a pre-law student at the University of Maryland, quickly and confidently snapped back, "I understand you, Chris," and put my tensions at ease.

I suspected that I was significantly misunderstood amongst everyone that was living in Beach City but a sharp, legal mind understood me. There were wild rumors circulating around the city that I had "gone crazy" and "lost my mind"—rumors which were only 1/3 true at best. The important fact that a sharp, pre-law student understood me, however, eased my worries about the flagrant misrepresentations of my character.

Now supported by a healthy dose of outside confidence, I chose to explore rather than party as we arrived at the Palace. Earlier, I had reached the clearing of the cave, but knew that I couldn't just stop there. I had to leave the cave and explore the side of Light because the clearing wasn't the real end of the Surf, but merely the catalyst of the rising Wave.

A group of atheists from the Catholic school Mount St. Mary's were hanging out at my house and I—re-born in Spirit, decided to preach to them. Girls, kegs, nightswimming—these were not the priorities at the moment. Dutifully relaying the good news was.

I was trying to convince these late teens that if they simply experienced the "warmth" of humanity they would believe in a higher power. I tried to appeal to them by explaining how dogmatic "religious" institutions could ironically serve as deterrents to belief in God. These kids told me that they grew up Catholic, couldn't accept the faith doctrine, and foolishly abandoned the Search.

"Listen, a religion dominated by fear is false. Jesus said "perfect love casts out fear" so don't let the hell-fire dogmas scare you from being human. Two, people that say they're religious and condescend people for not going to Church aren't truly religious because condescension is the exact *opposite* of what Jesus taught. Three, a lot of the Bible has been manipulated, words have been mistranslated, and political motives have influenced what has gone in it. Four, being religious is not believing in virgin births or Adam and Eve, it's loving your neighbor."

Although these kids were strangers, I cared for the well-being of their spiritual health. Rabid atheism, Nietzsche-style, from my experience is not in stride with reality and therefore a downward spiral to unhappiness. Nietzsche got laid one time in his life, by a hooker, and got a venereal disease from her that made him permanently insane until it killed him. One could say, in light of these facts, that I felt a "calling" to speak to them.

"Try to doing a good deed for a change and experience the awesome feeling of giving." I told them. "It's sublime! It goes beyond words and consider that your connection to the divine. Keep it simple. You don't have to believe stories that dictate 5700 years ago two naked people pissed off God and damned the human race. Take it figuratively. Why did Adam and Eve get kicked out of the Garden? They were embarrassed to be naked. Moral of the story…Don't be embarrassed to be naked! That's the true interpretation of the Creation story. We were created naked! And we weren't embarrassed. We weren't! God only got mad when Adam and Eve covered themselves up out of the embarrassment of being naked. Moral of the story, once again—don't be embarrassed to be naked."

I at least had their stoned attention, although I might not have changed their minds about the existence of God and the meaning of religion as I saw it. But I tried my best. I just felt a duty, in light of the fresh discoveries I had been guided to, to push others to a newer understanding of understanding of religion—one suited for a culture with so much information and resources at its fingertips.

As the night burned on, I think I made at least some progress in changing their skepticism of the presence of something beyond the human race. This was because I was speaking from legitimate experience, creatively interpreting Biblical stories, and preaching without dogma or judgment.

I eventually stopped with my "Experience the Warmth" sermon but not until light hit the earth. At this point I rushed to the beach in hope of watching the sun rise.

I told Dawkins and the other atheists that a sunrise in the Shinto context could be a deeply spiritual experience—a realization of the utter simplicity, yet beauty and glory of Creation. You had to live down the beach to know it as only those that saw it in such a context could know. I used that analogy with God.

"You can't really grasp what's meant by God until you feel the affections of love and discover how they root life in what really matters—friends, family, service. Once you do that, things start to make sense." I said I as I watched the sunrise on this early August day, the sun awake, the surfers engaged in their early morning "religious" ritual. Staring into the local waves, I drew symbolism from the surf.

In a purely poetic sense, the waves symbolized our *telos*. Telos is a term very important in philosophy. 1st applied by Aristotle, telos is the inherent principle of growth in created things as moved by Nature. Everything in Creation has a growth element or telos to it, from plants to people.

The board is our inner voice. This is a Gandhian term—roughly meaning our soul, or the part of us that feels the most real. If we listen to our inner voice, we can successfully surf the wave and grow into a fully realized human being because we'll be in tune with what's true in ourselves. But if we ignore it and live as motivated by gluttonous physical desires only, we'll fall off of our boards and drown before actualizing our potential because we'll be abandoning our true selves.

If we stay on our boards however, and listen to our inner voice despite the plethora of outside sounds, we will be rewarded with the satisfaction of being a complete person once we reach the shores.

My thinking was very figurative yet basic. It was derived from a real appreciation for simple, nature-deifying spiritualities like Shinto as well as the knowledge of Aristotle's brilliant insight that all things in nature have a telos. This comprehensible thought extended from the surf metaphor to my own recent re-generative experience, symbolized by the new day.

I was born-again. Not through Jesus Christ, per se, but through Grace. Not by the wrathful God of the Old Testament, but by the arbitrary hand of Noah's God of Love, I was given new life. This God was "ultimately real" to use a definition provided by the great philosopher Jacob Needleman, and her warmth felt like swimming in the August Atlantic water's on this pristine morning. I conceptualized the simple swim session as a sort of baptism.

When I was eight months I was baptized officially, but without my consent. I invited Jesus to be my personal Lord and Savior, committed to Catholicism, and received the sanctifying grace of Christ through the sacrament of baptism before I could even use words. Today I just baptized myself as a natural mystic, enlightened by love with a deep-seated yearning for what's true and beautiful.

When this unconventional ocean-side baptism was run dry, I walked back to the Palace where I saw Mary and her roommates in the parking lot getting ready to drive off into the morning light.

"Where are you girls going?" I naturally inquired.

"Oh well every summer since middle school we've volunteered with the Hope City Special Olympics. It's kind of a little tradition of ours and we certainly can't let a crazy summer like this one keep us from following it. So we're driving back home to help out with it." Mary informed me.

I had seen her last night, but was so deeply endowed to my preaching duties that I didn't pay attention to her. This was my mistake. Thankfully, it didn't seem to affect her. But then again, I didn't understand girls very well. So she could very well have been concealing some inner hurt.

"Mary's brother is special, Chris." Kristi added.

"Oh" I said, my stomach sinking, the right comment clouded by confusion. Mary had never mentioned that to me. Then grace.

"Well I think it's great you girls are doing this. You're not like most girls I know and I mean that in a good way. You're very well-rooted. You put others first. I think you have a good sense of what's important based on the small amount of time I've known you." I followed with typical virgin purity.

"Awww. Thanks Chris, you're sweet," Mary and Kristi answered, appreciative of the rare pure and innocent college guy.

"Is your brother competing?" I asked Mary.

"Yes. He got a silver medal in the long jump and a bronze in the 100 meter dash last year. So he's competing for the gold in those two events this year." Mary answered.

"Well I'm sure he'll be inspired by his little sister's cheers." I followed again in super-nice virgin style.

"I'm sure he will. My whole family will be there rooting for him and my friends." Mary replied with faith.

"Well I hope he gets the gold," I told Mary sincerely and virginally and wished them goodbye, genuinely impressed once again by the kindness of my Hope High School neighbors.

I walked up the beer can graced stairs to discover that Mark had also reaped the fruits of *his* search. I had embraced the mystery of the trinity, while he had successfully completed a threesome with two Catholic school girls, Melissa Hand and Julia Jobb.

I discovered the three Eckhart graduates sparsely clothed in his big, green bed when I entered Mark and Peter's tapestry laden room.

"Mark, you wanna go to McDonald's breakfast dude?" I asked just before I saw two half-naked girls around Mark's arms.

"Oh, I guess you're kind of tied up at the moment." I said answering my own question.

"Holy shit! Mark had a threesome!" I thought completely stunned but not surprised because after all, these girls *were* Catholic. I was delighted to see that Mark found what he was looking for and could rest with two girls in his bed after living the Office Space dream of "doing two chicks at the same time".

But although I had reached the clearing in the cave, I still didn't think my journey was over. After all, I had spent the night awake and preaching to stoned college kids. An enlightened person knows the importance of regular sleep and a journey always concludes with rest. Therefore, I couldn't consider my wave crashing/my journey over until regular sleep was once again a staple of my young life.

Mystery

"The Tao that can be told is not the eternal Tao"—Japanese proverb

A mighty wind blew into my surf when my parent's arrived in Beach City later in the day for our family vacation. Now, staying on my board and riding the wave with a Buddha smile would take extra concentration and effort. Two streams of thought were destined to intersect in an unhealthy manner. There was my parents' simple and healthier stream, adherent to the social norms, following the law and going with the organic flow. Then there was my eccentric stream, blazing its own course, listening to Nature, and trying to discover a new route to the limitless ocean of beauty.

One need not be a primary witness to appreciate the current dilemma. I was exploring uncharted territory spiritually and couldn't submit to my parent's or any authority for that matter's will. The only way I could truly become a man, as far as I believed, was to find a way to God for myself. My parents couldn't quite understand this fundamental fact but rightfully so. After all, not too many keg-standing nineteen year olds all of a sudden start to passionately yearn to make sense of life's greatest mysteries during a summer at the beach.

Despite the lack of precedent for my behavior though, it was undeniably presiding. I was now on a mission—sincerely pursuing higher truths, aspiring to have a symbolic vision, and while my body was here, my head was in a place only the mystic's have known.

I knew that I would come back down at some point, but as Kant argued, "In order to examine yourself, you have to exit yourself" and I truly was outside of my normal self, bound to the philosophical spirit of inquiry until forty days had passed. A green light was flashing across the bay and I was reaching out for it. I held biblical faith that I could grasp it.

* * *

I had been awake for a solid thirty hour span when my parents invited me to a family dinner in West Beach City. The inevitable result was a peaceful meal polluted with insomnia inspired ramblings.

Rather than venture into the depths of "religious" discovery at dinner, like they usually did, my comments stayed on a more local plane—my comedic assessment of the hardass. I started to tell our party how I was going to write this amazing piece of literature, a contemporary "Catcher in the Rye" entitled "Everybody Farts, Hardass" to cure society from its cancer of the hardass.

"Mom, Dad, Uncle Jesse, Aunt Becky, Steve, and DJ, there's no reason to be hardass if you're not struggling to survive or defending people's lives. So I'm writing a book to ridicule the hardass who doesn't meet these conditions. I am going to rip on groups like the "Metallica Rocks. DMB Sucks" Hardass, the "No Fun under 21. I'd card my own mother" Hardass and the "You only go to Church on Easter? You're going to hell" Hardass I really will. It's a problem and it's my God-given duty to change it. It's going to be like a new Catcher in the Rye." I said.

My uncle, a chemist, thought that I made a reasonable argument but noted the cold veracity that getting it published at nineteen would be extremely difficult. My father, a government official, elaborated on my uncle's argument, informing me that the publishing industry was too cutthroat to publish a nineteen year old's book, especially when its titled featured the word "fart".

In retrospect they both were right, but I was living in a highly Romanticized reality where anything was possible for this short period. It was a golden tinted reality where hope was the quintessential virtue and the God of Love was the Governor of Governor's. Thus, anything was possible here. Including a deep conversation with my Father.

After our comically charged seafood dinner, the family and I returned to our condo on 133rd street. At this point, night now spreading through the sky, my mind switched back to its deep, metaphysical mode.

My appetite for a real discussion with my Father inevitably translated into a Socratic Style Q and A session. He never tried discussing "the deep" with his Father but I wanted to break from that tradition. I was at a very important point in my life, a crossroads between childhood and adulthood where I needed a real connection to my Father. His mother had died shortly before the summer and I knew that deep down he was soulfully exploring the great planes of metaphysics because my mother had told me he was and I trusted my mother. My Father was searching deeply, looking to the great unknown for some sort of "spiritual healing" and my mother, a massage therapist, suggested that I talk to him about it. Therefore, I initiated an unprecedented discussion and asked my dad if he thought that the Counting Crows song "Anna Begins" was a symbol of the concept of "religious" re-generation—Re-birth. This was a very important theme in metaphysical literature. My hope was that by bringing up the "Born-Again" issue we could start to talk about other deep issues.

One of my dad's best friends had become "Born-Again" no later than three years ago. Also, President Rich—the most powerful man in the world and also the man whom my Father planned to vote for in the November election, said that Jesus was his favorite philosopher because he "changed his heart". When asked to elaborate, President Rich said, "I can't really describe it. It's too great to be spoken. It's one of those things that you can only know if you experience it."

President Rich's re-birth clearly went beyond words and gave him new life as a "Born-Again Christian". In an Eastern lens of understanding, although most Americans including Rich would never picture it way, it was the "True Tao"—that which cannot be spoken. Regardless of what terminology you use however, my president, my Father's friend, and I both had similar "new life" experiences and therefore made the discussion relevant.

I spoke of my uplifting experiences to my Father and he assured me, practical and wise as he was, "It was a new beginning."

Then I started talking about the film The Matrix and the concept of the ONE. My Father said, "Trust me, you're not the messiah."

"Well maybe it's like Emerson said and we all have the potential to messiahs or saviors if we let God work through us, trust ourselves, and live to our full potential." I countered, anticipating the natural response of shock.

I believed, and forgive me for being anti-historical but here it goes, that the spirit of Jesus—a divine light, could shine in *each and every* genuine God seeker and, in this sense, enable a bounty of anointed ones. Not to say that anyone could match Jesus in power of message, of life, in insight, in meaning, in sacrifice, in Truth; rather that people who seek God could become beacons of his light too, however tiny. Regardless, even by my definition, I couldn't claim to be a messiah, although I did consider God's grace to be a loyal helper in my life.

Such theological thinking was all so heavy, but again, as I've tried to explain, I had been very pious in my youth. This early piety, I am certain played a crucial role in laying the foundation for the great voyage of discovery I experienced in my later teens. Without it, I probably would have been a wandering agnostic, unmedicated, faithless, and in serious coping troubles with my mysterious condition as a result. But with it, I had the faith that I needed to triumph over whatever trials and troubles the mysterious condition would bring me.

As a child, I wore my scapula with pride, didn't curse, prayed often, always did the right thing, and saw the world as I was told to see it—filled with sin and only healed by the Greater Grace of God as administered through the Sacraments. As I grew older and more skeptical, however, I started to doubt the certainty of the Catholic dogma, mostly because I thought that it failed to capture the heart of Jesus' message. Christ's key commandments were "Love your Lord your God with all your heart, all your mind, and all your soul. Love your neighbor as yourself." Not "Attend Mass every Sunday or go to Hell." Not "Say forty Hail Mary's for every time you've played with your wiener in the last month."

A disillusioned late teen, I also started to see the beginning of the end of the Catholic church's dominance—the priest pedophilia scandals (1 out 20 Priests), The Da Vinci Code, Post-Modernism, decline in church attendance (10% of American Catholics attend Church regularly), destruction of dogma, and considered the possibility that divine providence had eased the dead-lock grip that the Catholic Church had once held so firmly on Truth. Then I heard a speech courtesy of Harvard educated philosopher, Samuel Yeshua.

Yeshua had been surveying the religious traditions of the world for over forty years and when asked after this long search which religion he identified with he said, "Some concepts of Zen Buddhism."

Judging by the mesmerizing effect of his speech and the upward intuitive sway of his profound insight, I concluded this man was a genius. Since he was so, I knew I had to take his message to heart and never forget the part of the speech that he emphasized the most—its ending. The ending of Yeshua's transformative speech was a story, one that he considered among his personal favorites.

The story was very simple but incredibly inspirational at the same time. It was about a little boy in Mexico who had to give away his favorite toy to a beggar. The boy naturally was hesitant but eventually followed through with his Father's will. After giving away his favorite toy the boy, overcome by joy, ran back in the house exclaiming, "Daddy, Daddy can I do that again??!!"

Dr. Yeshua was a brilliant man in his seventies, educated at Harvard and Yale, and he considered *this* one of his favorite stories. The fact that a man of his wisdom and learning did so, served as a testament to the story's truth-value in my opinion.

My Father eventually grew slightly irritated by my hippie philosophizing and said, "I like having intellectual discussions with you but I could never have these kinds of discussions with my Father."

He reasoned that because his he and his Father never discussed the sacred mysteries of life that he and his son couldn't. I believed that lack of precedent is not a legitimate reason for abandoning an activity, but my Father's rule was sovereign, a conversation could not continue solo, and perhaps he was wise in his wish to keep the Father/son conversation free from intellectual abstraction.

Before I went to bed, I thought about my Father's wisdom and flirted with the possibility that maybe the sacred mysteries of faith were meant to be left alone—that my Father was speaking from life experience when he told me that my recent moments signaled a new beginning but nothing further. It was wisdom that sobered me up, at least for the moment.

Youth

"Youth comes but once in a lifetime"—Longfellow

Inspired by my Father's call to let the sacred mysteries be, I had an epiphany—"maybe, just maybe," I considered, "19 year old, 21st century American males living at the beach for the summer with their friends weren't *meant* to be esthetic theologians. Rather they were meant to be fun-loving teenagers celebrating their youth."

Despite the beautiful bliss my condition was propelling me towards—a beautiful bliss engaged to profound senses of a higher calling, I accepted this insight as the gospel truth. Therefore, if only for the moment, I came back down to reality as defined by the collegiate culture that ran the Pink Palace—a reality defined by kegs, high school girls, and ten cup Ruit. I would fly back through the atmosphere again and soar to what Plato called the "form world" very quickly because of a shocking truth revealed.

As of the present moment however, I was getting low, loving life, and living the teenage dream once again. Now tilted toward earth, I considered the mysteries of faith too perplexing. The finite human mind, as I now viewed it, couldn't possibly wrap itself around the God's infinite wisdom. Because it couldn't, I now deemed my best strategy to get Epicurean by eating, drinking, and being merry.

In tune with this revived hedonism, I started partying Teen Wolf style—large and in charge, at our fabulous Pink House for the first time in three weeks. I was taking forty second Natty Light keg stands, playing Ruit on the turf dressed table, and actually being a teenager one sticky August night when I decided to stumble outside. My good friends were out on the deck reflecting on our collegiate lifestyle and I was an avid talker so naturally I eased my way into the discussion. We started to sling commentary back and forth about our decaying lifestyle.

"Dude our house is a mess. The bathroom still has Scott's shit-filled diaper in it from the diaper party. The fly traps don't even have any more room for flies!" John exclaimed.

"Yeah dude, and we've gotten drunk every night for like three straight months. I haven't had a solid shit all summer, Castile has serious kidney problems." Peter followed.

"Yeah, maybe people weren't meant to live like pigs." I chimed in.

"Yeah, definitely. This summer's been a real shit show." John replied. Then Mark stumbled out on the deck.

"Where's Mary?" He inquired.

Mark saw all of her roommates outside with us but Mary was missing. We all quickly shrugged our shoulders. Well everyone except John. He knew and froze.

When the moment was silent, John took a careful pause, looked around as a poetic device, and then in a genuinely crude tone answered, "She's downstairs fucking Jack!"

"She's downstairs fucking Jack??!!" I asked semi-rhetorically with a heavy dose of shock.

"Yeah dude. Sorry you had to find out this way." John nodded disappointedly.

"This doesn't make fucking sense dude." I snapped back, pulling my shaggy, brown hair back in ineffable surprise.

"Mary's not as innocent as she seems, Chris. Remember, she told the lifeguard Tim that she wanted to be sexually free this summer? When I told you that it was *meant* to be a hint, you idiot! She's been trying to hook up with you all summer, but you've been so far in outer space to notice her signals." John informed me.

"No, you're fucking with me dude," I followed not yet ready to embrace the naked truth.

"No I'm not, remember when she came into the Ruit Room all dressed up wearing sweet, Abercrombie perfume in a white sundress and you decided to preach to the Mount St. Mary's kids instead?...She was trying to get you to notice her and you just fucking ignored her. You just fucking ignored her and it broke her heart. She got ready for an hour just for you and fell to her knees on the deck and cried when you ignored her. She was balling her eyes out while you were preaching about God knows what to those Mount St. Mary's kids. That was fucked up dude. Or how about when she stood outside our room let down her hair and looked you in the eyes and you just rolled over in fucking bed on our Fourth of July party? Or when she tried to freak with you on the dance floor on your birthday and you just walked away?" John answered authoritatively. "Girls like you to pay attention to them. Haven't you learned anything?" He followed.

"But dude, I did all that because I have no fucking confidence with girls, I have none! I made out with one girl one time. I've had no practice. No fucking practice. So when a girl like Mary comes around I really want to please her, but because I don't have any hook-up experience am afraid to. I'm afraid. Ok are you happy now? I'm afraid! Not to stand up to police, not to be different. Not to pursue the meaning of life. Not to buy beer underage. But to hook up with a girl that I am attracted to. It's messed up man. I guess I am always waiting for the Office Space Christmas Night moment and not content with random Sin City loving. I don't know dude, if I would have just made moves when I was younger, I'd have the experience I needed to feel confident today. But I didn't and the more time passes the more unconfident I get. It's a vicious cycle, bro. Natural though. And another thing. I understand, thanks to what you told me, how I did Mary wrong. And believe me, I'm really gonna regret it. But Jack? C'mon. That's a little unnecessary. I'd feel a lot better if it were you or Peter or even Mark, but Jack? He's an animal, he's only after sex. He walks around like he's Sean Bateman from the Rules of Attraction and always is saying "figure it out, deal with it". But not Mary. She acts like a sincere Christian and is nice to everybody. She has a bleeding heart and is always filled so much positivity. She doesn't say "figure it out, deal with it" but instead helps people with their problems." I sobbed.

"Still, that doesn't mean she's not horny dude. Maybe you should stop being all philosophical and shit, accept your culture and hook up with chicks. It's a lot of fun, dude. Trust me." John responded.

"Ok fine. I can appreciate that advice." I relayed back. "But she invited me to meet the Christian missionaries that she was entertaining at her house the other day. I think it's reasonable for me to be shocked that she would give up her body for a dooshbag like Jack only a couple of weeks later." I said.

"Touché. But Jack does have a reputation for attracting chicks, dude. He got with a lot of hot girls in high school, you know. They all thought he was hot and he had the game to go with it. Mary fell for a trap many, many before have fallen into. He probably slung a lot bullshit to her like he did to them. Like he probably told her she was beautiful and special and shit, and obviously it worked. Plus Mary, she's only eighteen and Jack's twenty, so he has that older guy appeal. People make mistakes sometimes. Especially involving the rules of attraction. That's why you forgive, homie." John replied.

"You're right. And that's why she deserves forgiveness. Also, I made a big mistake by ignoring her. I bet that hurt her just as much as me finding out about Jack. Maybe. And it's ultimately up to God to forgive. But still—Jack *is* making Mary moan and sweat as we speak." I said as I pictured the unfortunate mental imagery that I'll spare you from translating for the sake of decency.

"This little girl whom I'd poured my heart to was truly not as pure as she appears." I conceded accepting my bitter defeat at the sneaky hands of Jack.

Despite John's wise words, my heart snapped in two as it had when I found out about Elizabeth and I started to feel ill. I was, once again, dealt a horrible dose of an unforeseen sexual reality—the story of my life.

"And they have been fucking *all summer* in secret." John added to reflect reality, enhance the argument, and unintentionally make the wound a little bit deeper.

Naturally, I sunk into melancholy. Jack didn't deserve Mary's body really. He was boning three other girls not including his girlfriend without Mary's knowledge. But lust is such a powerful drug that it can destroy Reason.

"Living on 39th street really is like Lord of the Flies." I concluded. "Hedonism collapses the rule of order."

"Sometimes Mary does things when she's drunk that she wouldn't do when she's sober," our neighbor and Mary's roommate Kristi added in her defense.

I momentarily ignored her justification because if they'd been doing it all summer, there had to be at least a couple sober sessions. Maybe. Although as I thought about the issue more, I considered the possibility that perhaps this really wouldn't be something that Mary would do sober. At this point in the summer at least.

In the last two weeks, Mary had witnessed Jack try to fight the lost Mexican, rage against my preaching self, and kick harmless Pietro out of *my* house. Also, she had heard that he had been in two real fights—one in the McDonald's corridor (the little space in between the first entrance and restaurant entrance) and another on 73rd street with her cousin's boyfriend.

So maybe, after seeing his ugly underside, she wouldn't spoon with him sober. Later I found out that she used to be really attracted to Jack but as the summer went on and she got to know him, that attraction faded. But when she got drunk those horny hormones sometimes took over. So Kristi's interpretation was accurate. Regardless, the incident sent me back into the clouds for an answer. I walked forty yards out to the beach alone and reflected in the ominously pale moonlight.

"Maybe this was the end of my ride on the Great Wave," I first thought as I watched the little Beach City waves crash on the sands. "A crude, nihilistic, but realistic discovery that human beings ultimately crave sexual fulfillment most and that dick size is more important than heart size as a result. Maybe that's the way reality truly was and I had just been escaping it all my life out of prudeness and naivety. Because, after all, Elizabeth did put an acne dick in her mouth on New Year's and let some Latin guy fingerblast her. Because, after all, Jack and Mary were spooning for the majority of the summer whether they were drunk or sober.

These were the hard facts, *a posteriori*—or as the scientific community understands it, "in accordance with reality." Therefore they were inescapable.

I was fixated on that idea until some insight. "Patience Christopher" my inner voice told me as I gazed in wonder at the glowing, August moon.

"Maybe this was a sign that Mary was nothing more than a simple crush and Elizabeth was the real prize, or better yet, that the best is yet to come," I thought. "Maybe you should be kind to everyone though because it's tough to be human and everyone deserves a break. So go back to the Palace and wish them the best," the wind of my soul told me. I listened. Because I did, I went back to talk to those two recent love makers after forty minutes of deliberation on the night beach.

Mary and Jack on the 2nd floor talking on our deck. They were both sweaty. Mary's hair was all over the place.

"I just wanted to say, I'm happy for you guys." I said using all of the strength generated during my ocean front session, trying to put a positive spin on the situation.

"No" Mary said instinctively. "Jack and I talked. We're too different to keep doing what we were doing," she replied, looking deeply remorseful, like she was now completely aware of her behavior. This was more like the Mary I had grown to know over these past two months—always aware of the smart choice.

Jack and Mary continued talking despite my presence and Jack looked really infuriated. He consented to a summer sex session—not to a post-game interview to supplement it. Impatient as a terrible two year old, Jack protested as Mary, in his view, wasted his sacred time talking with him. Mary asked Jack, "Do you believe in helping other people?"

"No" Jack snapped back as if it were a ridiculous notion.

"Well I do. That's why I volunteer and try to do nice things for everybody, especially friends and family." Mary replied.

"Why you still talking? I thought this was over. You don't want to fuck me anymore, so why are we still talking?" Jack said back to Mary. Mary looked so crushed, salty tears gently streaming down her sun-baked skin. What started out as just some healthy teenage fun had turned into instant scar tissue.

I walked back into the Pink Palace shaking my head, dumb, damaged, drained but still thankful that Mary had finally seen the situation in the white light, painful as it was for her. Lying in bed, fading everything into black and blue, I spent yet another night alone. I didn't sleep, I didn't stop thinking, and when I finally crashed, the sun had already risen.

Sin

"People are sinnin', Satan's grinnin"—Evangelical Proverb

39th Street. Beach City, Maryland. August 13, 2004.

Seeking recovery, I peace rolled with Mark to my first Roller Dough party in nearly a month. I hadn't seen any of the other employees since that strange Sunday when I began to change. Therefore, I hoped that attending the party would be therapeutic for me and educational for them.

I believed that partying and loving life would be a welcome vacation from philosophical speculation for me as well as a valid way to show the Roller Dough crew who I really was—a good kid who thinks no doubt, but also likes to celebrate life and certainly not an abstractly speaking insomniac who has a problem with everyone that's not deep. It was a hope that would be justified.

Upon our Natty Light 30-rack graced entrance to the 55th street fiesta, Mark and I jumped on the Ruit table and instantly began to dominate. Our endless nightly sessions of ten cup Ruit translated into a stellar performance on this six cup table. Each of the house residents was legitimately impressed by our skill but eventually two Beach City locals ran Mark and me off the table.

Shocked from our unlikely defeat, I stumbled through the party absolutely speechless until a profound image captured my blurred attention. It was an image that pulled my philosophical spirit up from hibernation for the moment—the crystallized sight of one of my former co-workers, Adam, staring off into space in an almost trance-like state.

A life-long hippie, Adam was the one that informed me on the wild July workday that I was "Speaking like the Buddha". Adam was the only one that really understood the power of my speech.

When I walked over to Adam as he sat quietly on a chair with an awestruck outerspace stair, he slowly looked over at me and whispered secretively, "I'm never doing drugs again." Naturally, I asked why because Adam always did drugs.

"You ever heard that Dave Matthews song, Too High?" Adam asked.

"Yeah. Of course." I answered.

Alex paused, looked around the room, and said with a cosmic smile, "It's all energy," as if he could feel all the energy generated around us.

Leaning back in his chair, smiling like the Awakened One, Adam had discovered the secret garden of enlightenment. Therefore, he felt the need never to do drugs again. I could identify with him—seeing the light is pretty mind blowing when you first see it, way better than any drug. But after you see the light, I believe, it's your duty to help others see it to.

After talking hippie with Alex, I was now able to booze and live like a teenager with most of the former employees once again because I had my Eastern philosophy fix for the day. The Roller Dough kids and I drank booze from the fountain of youth and celebrated life in Beach City. We shotgunned and bonged Natty Light's, slapped fives, and engaged in fierce wrestling matches.

"Chris the Tank, Chris the Tank" the kids kept chanting as I bonged out of the three-beer funnel. My former co-workers were clearly glad to see that I was healthy, or at least better, and the storm of intense revival had calmed.

Following another hour of quarters, flip cup, and Ruit, I passed my old manager Michael, not the boss, but second in command on my way out of the keg cap plastered door. Eight years my senior, Michael really worried about me on that epic Sunday and wanted to make sure that I was doing ok, saying, "I hope you can pass off your last day as a *learning experience,*" emphasizing learning.

"Yeah, it really was a learning experience." I responded truthfully. I was only nineteen and thus still had a lot about life to learn. Ten minutes later, I would learn another important life lesson—girls don't react fondly to getting played. I would have known this earlier, if only I was so fortunate to learn it from life experience.

Boldly belligerent, Frank the Tank style—Mark and I stumbled on the bus and rode it back to 39th street. We conversed with the drunken forty year-old women coming from Seacrets as usual on the bus. "You boys looking for a good time?" The veteran skuzzers asked us.

"Of course," we responded playing their typical game.

"I just got divorced from my husband…" one of them informed us. Not a surprise.

"Uh, we gotta go," we told the horny forty year olds and arrived on Thirty-Ninth Street with one eye open soon after.

When we did, complete chaos was erupting and Lord of the Flies parallels were becoming real as a result. Mary and another one of Jack's former girls were spelling out "MANWHORE" in shaving cream on the pavement while he was busy giving the time to another girl, Gina.

Apparently, these two girls who Jack both made it seem like were the only ones had witnessed Jack porking Gina by looking through the window outside his house. The bitter reality that they were being "played" sunk in and they reacted impulsively by spelling MANWHORE in shaving cream on the street corner.

The played girls left an angry message on Jack's phone to the tune of, "Jack, you're a complete scumbag. I hope you get herpes with that whore," and the younger one—Alison, went up on my deck for Jack counseling. She was seventeen.

I told Alison that Jack was going through a rough time in his life and to not let his actions get her down. She replied by saying sorrowfully, "Jack made it seem like it was just me and him."

"I'll say something to him." I vowed to the high schooler.

Jack pimp strolled outside after his session of summer sex to see, first hand, that he was a manwhore. Unamused by the aesthetic display that gently graced the summer sidewalk though, Jack started yelling and screaming at the young girls in a fiery pitch.

"Fuck you, girls. You wanted to fuck me. Don't try and be all innocent."

Even though I half agreed with Jack, I stayed faithful to my word.

"Jack, remember you said, "Figure it out, deal with it?" I yelled down to him.

"Yeah" Jack said while he turned his head to Mary, "Yeah figure it out, deal with it," he said right before I quickly cut-him off.

"Well *you* need to figure it out and deal with it. *You* need to respect women!" I asserted down to him.

I think Jack busted a couple of blood vessels trying unsuccessfully to fathom the situation. All those that surrounded him were against him including his guy friend. I never felt guilty about being against him though—I pretty much hated him at this point in the summer.

"Fuck you Chris, you crazy mother fucker. I hope you burn in hell with your bullshit philosophies," the Irishman roared back red-eyed.

"Ok buddy." I said sarcastically and continued to sit silently on a tacky wooden chair known as the "Omega" chair. A throwback to the late 1970's, it was known as the Omega chair because its back resembled the last letter of the Greek alphabet. It also had symbolic value because these times were the Omega—the last, of days.

I let the parties argue further as I sat supported by the Omega chair, pondering the strange events that comprised my summer. Once again, despite my youth, I was back in meditative mode.

Rocket Summer

In the beginning of the summer, life was much simpler. I wasn't searching for answers and starving for truth. I was closer to where my college life started, playing lots of Ruit. I wasn't suffering from a lonely heart, my favorite people surrounded me. I wasn't fighting with my friends—I was getting blitzed and laughing alongside them. And most importantly, I wasn't staying up for days.

I slept every single night with sand in my bed, Pizza Tugos in my hand, for the 1st two months of the summer. So I longed for those glory days when things weren't so crazy. The beginning of the summer was simpler, but what I really yearned for was days like the first summer living at the beach—my first before college.

During that sun-centered summer, I worked the night shift at the Greene Turtle restaurant and bar. My job was simply to guard the beer in the outside coolers and I had mastered it in a matter of hours.

After I worked that job from 9-3, I rode my bike home, played Tiger Woods Golf till sunrise, slept till 5 p.m., partied before work, and went back to guarding the beer. The Change hadn't occurred hence I couldn't have been happier and mentally healthier. My life was simple and I hadn't taken a philosophy class. Therefore, I was pretty normal.

Now however, I was without work, struggling with the deepest existential questions, and starting to get very sick. I looked ahead to an uncertain future to see a world of 9-5's and was scared, especially because the innocence of the times was quickly lost. Everybody was preoccupied with sex, a mystery to me. The fact that I never had it instilled a curiosity within so itchy that it was starting to cause illness.

Ugly CCD teachers told me that sex was "the greatest thing in the world" but emphasized the necessity of abstinence until marriage. My peers made it seem like it was also the greatest thing in the world but not being married didn't stop them from thoroughly enjoying it.

I continued, despite the ongoing drama outside, to reflect on my summer and how much it changed me. My perspective was so much different driving to the beach from Sacred Heart in May of 2004. Then, my biggest worry was whether or not I would be able to use my Fake ID, not whether or not Jesus was coming back! Then, I wanted to try to hook-up with girls, not naively attach myself to them emotionally. Then, I wanted to reach thirty seconds on a Keg stands, not *nirvana.* But, as I grew to realize, sometimes things happen for a reason and perhaps these changes were part of a master plan that God—a supreme intelligence far greater than me, had spawned.

Critically examining myself, I recognized a side that wished I never went on this philosophical journey. There was a real side that wished that I stayed in a state of equilibrium throughout the summer instead. But I also recognized another side, a side stronger and braver, that said, Rounders style, "You can't lose what you don't put in the middle...But you can't win much either." This courageous side wanted me to reach for angels, it wanted the answers to life's biggest puzzles, and it wanted to know the nature of God because it sought primetime knowledge.

* * *

In the midst of all my summertime reflections, I saw an angel with broken wings walking up the stairs to our deck. She looked really upset—I could read the emotion it in her eyes. Mary looked as if she were about to do something that would be very, very painful for her to do—something she didn't want to do, but felt that she had no choice but to do. Sympathizing with Mary's soulful sadness, I significantly amplified the depth of my mood to connect with her.

"How you doing, Mary?" I said softly, slowly.

"Not Good Chris." Mary replied just about to weep like a dumped middle school girl. She paused to withhold her youthful tears and after the collectively somber moment ended, she said as quickly and as difficultly as possible, "Goodbye Chris" with a light slide of sorrow slowly slipping down her face as she walked away to her 1st floor apartment.

"Good Night." I said softly as Mary hurried downstairs, hopeful that we would see each other again.

"Mary's really embarrassed about the whole Jack thing, Chris. She thinks really highly of you and with all of this drama happening, doesn't think you want anything to do with her. Especially because she keeps trying to be intimate with you and you keep ignoring her. She can heal you Chris. She has a gift. But now, I think she's going home for the summer. It really ended sadly for her. Maybe she should have done Young Life." Mary's roommate and best friend Kristi informed me as we shared a Natty Light on the deck moments later.

"Kristi. I still think really highly of Mary. Really high. And the only reason why I ignored her is because I felt kind of intimated. I mean I have no hook-up practice so I don't want to embarrass myself with her. Also, she's one of the nicest people I've ever met and I know it's not easy being a girl nowadays either. So I want to keep talking to her."

"How do you know that? How could you know what it's like to be a girl nowadays?" Kristi asked.

"I watch people. I read people. I remember a lot of things. It's pretty much the same everywhere. No Romance. Guys think every girl is just for sex. Girls are mean as hell to each other. Society makes girls unhappy with their God-given beauty."

"Jesus, Chris. You really do pay attention! You don't get mad easy. You treat women with respect. You're not like most guys I know." Kristi replied just before we were rudely interrupted.

"Fuck you Chris," the Manwhore told me—a common theme of the summer.

"Kristi, go downstairs please. This could get ugly." I replied.

Kristi followed my instructions and then Jack got closer and started staring me down, full of anger, like a primal savage.

"Are you a fucking cave man or something? You think that stare down shit works on me? You think I'm going be a "man" and fight you right now? Fuck you manwhore!' I shouted at Jack.

"Fuck you Chris, you don't know anything about girls because you've never fucked before...you think Mary likes you??!!" Jack shouted at me.

The scene reminded me of Lord of the Flies when the character Simon is confronted by Lord of the Flies who tempts his faith.

"Yeah actually I do think Mary likes me, maybe not sexually, but she definitely likes me. She cried when she said goodbye to me. And you can leave you piece of shit. Why did you move in below us anyway? None of us ever liked you." I dictated to the red-faced Irishman.

Jack however, refused to follow house instructions. He just stood there staring at me like a hunter stares at his prey, ready to pounce. If I made one move that suggested I wanted to fight him, Jack would have quickly swung. But instead of swinging, I got Gandhi, refused violence and went back to bed. Like my father said, "it takes a bigger man to walk away from a fight" and with all Jack said to me all summer, not swinging at him justified that proverb. In my room I prayed.

"God, what is happening?" I asked in my night-time prayer. "In the beginning was peace—now chaos. If you're so loving and omnipotent God, why is there so much chaos in the world? Terrorism, Torture, Rape,

Murder, Hatred, how can you let this stuff happen? Why is this world so fucked up, God?"

Still, no matter how much darkness I was aware of, I couldn't let it blind me to the world radiant with the great light of love. Maybe the Daoists had the best sense of the nature of the world. Darkness balanced by light. Evil balanced by Good. And maybe my mission was to help be light to counter the darkness. Regardless, the care and compassion of my friends and family, the feeling derived from helping others—these affections could not go forgotten no matter how much darkness I saw. My figurative Wave had not reached the shores quite yet, despite my born-again spirituality and focusing on the dark side of humanity was a sign that would drown before I could reach it. As I struggled to reach the surface, I saw up in the illuminated night sky, the figure of Mr. Triumphant who brought me out the waters. I believed that Mr. Paul had a pure grasp of the true nature of Jesus.

He shaped his life around the Biblical Christ and built churches in his Glory. Jesus was not only Mr. Triumphant's inspiration—he was his guide to the Purpose Driven Life. Mr. Paul's heart beat to the rhythm of Jesus Christ. More passionately than any other man I had met. That's why at this young age I was so inspired by him.

I could now relate to him when he said, "I wrote that paper at a point in my life when I was seeing God in everything." And after he died on June 3rd, 2003 I started, at age of seventeen, to examine the earthly phenomenon known as "Life". What drives it? What gives it meaning? What's its purpose? And I looked no further than Mr. Triumphant for answers. Truly this man knew the purpose driven life as evident by his actions and wisdom—actions like founding a local chapter of the American Family Association, building churches, leading an altruistic family and Wisdom like, "Everybody deserves a second chance", "Don't stop giving", "Put women first."

Forgiveness

"The weak can never forgive. Forgiveness is the attribute of the strong"
—Gandhi

I rolled out of my big blue bed and into the Natty Light case dressed living room the next morning where I was instantly bombarded with juvenile grief. "Chris, I can't believe you took that girl's side over Jack's." Mark said to me.

"Are you kidding me? He broke a seventeen year old girls' heart, of course I'm not going to take his side. Especially after the way he's been treating me all summer—he's been like that kid from problem child." I replied.

"You took a girl's side over one of your friend's." Mark tried to explain to me.

"Well the way if he treats me, I took a girl's side over one of my enemies." I said back. Mark didn't feel the need to respond.

The day was gloomy—rainy and overcast, and as a result, the inspiration of serious inactivity. Jobless for nearly a month now, if I hadn't been accruing wisdom then I could have been accurately construed as a completely converted Beach bum. The truth of the matter was however, that no matter how out of sync with the real nature of things my immediate insights may have been, they were still the product of a heart and head hard at work. And that's why despite the fact that I didn't have a job, I was still working.

So when my roommates returned from bussing tables later in the day and teased me for being a bum, I fought back.

"Dude, thinking hard is harder than bussing tables. I think hard about life all day and I'm going to write a book about this summer." I said to John and Mark.

"Ok, Danielle Steele, hit this bowl." John instructed me.

Mary Cooper was still heavy on my half-baked head at the time, and although I knew that if I got really blazed the weight of my thoughts might collapse my creative awareness, I smoked bud anyway. The power of peer pressure is colossal, and the philosopher's urge to color his mind green is pretty potent.

As my neurons started slow and distort my perception of Time, I began to do some deep thinking on the issue of Mary, carefully weighing the pros and cons of meeting her.

On the very positive side, Mary Cooper truly was the owner of a big, happy heart and did a lot of great things for people. She volunteered, always gave kind words, and was consistently looking out for others. She loved her parents and read the Purpose Driven Life. We had very interesting, deep, and diverse talks and were becoming good friends until she say goodbye. Also, she considered me her "favorite" out of all the boys that lived above her as we caught her saying on video when she was drunk. For all these reasons and more, I was glad to be her friend.

On the negative side, she invited me to meet Christian missionaries one day, but was having sex with Jack all summer. And was pretty sneaky about it. Also, the whole Mark thing didn't make me happy and chipped away at my self-esteem. Therefore, I think meeting Mary did some damage to my mental health.

The green light verdict though, was that it was worth it. I realized, in the green light, that whatever darkness Mary's hook-ups with Mark and Jack brought me, the light that shined brilliantly from her diamond soul gave me a bounty of hope, of inspiration, of faith, of warmth that easily overshadowed it. I realized, in the green light, that it's foolish to assume that human beings are perfect—we're imperfect by design. That's why we must forgive and know people by their content of character—not quantity of youthful indiscretions. Therefore, I realized, in the green light, that I should forgive Mary as she would forgive me and think of her as a sweet young lady. I realized, in the green light, that girls go through phases in their life where the "bad boy" is attractive and the "great guy" is a huge tool. Therefore, I realized, in the green light, that I should stay faithful to my convictions and wait for the girls to come around to the bright side. And I realized, in the green light, that I was really freaking hungry.

A bag of buds now up in smoke, the time to devour munchies had naturally struck. Mark, owner of God's green gift to the earth, decided that he wanted to go Wendy's just outside of town to satisfy his fast-food craving.

"Mark, why don't we just go to Johnny's I's? We can walk there." I suggested, our safety my key concern.

"*I* wanna go to Wendy's," he stuttered, oblivious to the safety barren nature of his wish. "Let me drive your car." Mark insisted.

There was a very slim chance, about as slim as Ally McBeal, that I would let Mark, stoned and a dangerous driver even while sober, drive my mother's car.

"Be patient my son." I told Mark, knowing intuitively that the virtue of the wise would be rewarded. At the present, although Mark was a good kid, genuine in his faith, he still didn't quite get it. I, on the other hand, had finally bloomed. Consequently, we held divergent ideas about the best decision for our group.

In the thick of our fruitless debate—which mainly consisted of Mark badgering me to let him drive my mother's car and me telling him "No", a familiar but unexpected face appeared at the door.

Mary wandered meekly over into the 2nd floor of the Palace for a "Hello".

"Mary, I thought you left?" John said.

"Well, I just had dinner with my parents and they thought it would be a good idea to come back and reconcile." She replied.

Mary and I hadn't seen each other since she tearily told me "Goodbye". So when she visited us unsuspectingly, I became very relieved that my hope that the Manwhore night truly didn't mean goodbye forever was not in vain. Regardless, there was a somewhat awkward, unspoken vibe between us.

We truly needed to talk in order to relay our complicated feelings, but suffered from a communication breakdown recently following the ordeal with Jack and the Manwhore night. Combined with my sporadic bouts of extreme thought-flight and our collective lack of sobriety in the backdrop of an excess of sexual confusion, the foundations for intense drama were in place.

"Mary can drive us to Wendy's." John asserted, completing the patience puzzle. Naturally, Mary, always serving others, agreed.

John called "Shotgun" and joined Mark and I as Mary drove us to the West Beach City Wendy's for some well-earned munchies.

As I slyly slipped into Mary's green Volvo, my sandal strapped foot slid into a thick book. After I adjusted my position to co-exist with the book, I tilted my heavy head downward to discover its title. The title was "Shahid" and was about the women and children of Islam—the real holy martyrs and the faithful that suffer because of the sovereign rule of fanatical fairies that call themselves men.

Seeing this book in Mary's car gave me a deep-seated peace as it signaled that Mary had a great sense of what was important in global issues. The sight also instilled a well-grounded sense of respect, pride, and admiration for Mary in light of her efforts to understand and educate herself about this controversial yet widely misunderstood faith.

As we left behind the bright city lights of Beach City, John, on the hunt for mood-suiting music, discovered some CD's he had never encountered that also made me proud when their genre was revealed. An avid music listener, John was naturally curious about the style of music of these unknown artists.

"Mary, what are these CD's?" he asked. Mary just laughed.

"Oh, you guys don't want to listen to those, they are my *personal* CD's."

"Personal CD's?" John inquired with a dose of confusion.

"They're Christian CD's, John." Mary said.

"Mary, I think it's really awesome that you have those CD's." I replied religiously from the back seat. Mary was too humble to respond.

John, aware of the budding energy, said "Mary, you know, Chris used to be able to run like eight miles non-stop in high school."

He believed that Mary and I could have easily had a physical relationship this summer if I wasn't so fat/inactive and wanted to include that key fact about an earlier stage of my life. He also did this in order to portray a truer picture of the real Christopher Castile.

Mary responded seeking a similar effect by saying, "Well, in High School, I didn't play sports during the last two years because I did the Rock and Roll Revival with my mom which was a musical tour celebrating the Gospels of Jesus."

Again, I was delighted, but not surprised by this revelation. Mary really did have something special about her and I, unlike some of the Palace goers who only stared at her rack and never got to know her, knew this.

From my perspective, Mary had in an idealistic sense, the burning heart of a lion nestled inside the graceful outward beauty of an angel. In a realistic sense, she had a big heart, a hot body, a great smile, and a penchant for both personal pleasure and service. However, she wasn't absolutely certain that her true picture was being revealed. She was right—in the midst of a drunken, Animal House culture all that's really remembered by the heathens is a perverted exaggeration of the real—who she opened up to in a physical sense. But in the reality, it's a mosaic of many elements from their hook-ups to their halos that form the True Picture of a human being. Fortunately, I realized this and saw Mary in a brighter, more accurate light than most of the fratastic Palace goers.

When we reached West Beach City's Wendy's, Mark, John, and I raced for the register. 1950's Love Songs serenaded the atmosphere, making the meal especially Romantic for a fast food free for all.

"Oh my God, I love these songs." Mary said after a run of Stand by Me, Dream Lover, and This Magic Moment.

"Me too!" I responded, I was being honest. I used to drive home from school everyday at Eckhart these types of songs. "Things were different back then. Guys respected women and class was common."

John, still aware of the sublime energy, looked over at Mary and said, "How are you doing, Juliet?" thus causing her an unintended concern. Mary knew that Romeo and Juliet was a tragic love story. Hence, she didn't know how to interpret John's careful words. Mary looked over at me and I was so nervous and confused that I was shaking.

"Let's go. I'm done my meal" Mark said. I rolled my eyes and we all left for the Pink Palace.

On the way, a set of value meals now actively clogging our arteries, the confusion thickened and the collective mood started to go slightly mad as a result. Leaving the inlet bridge, Mary suddenly sneezed and John said "Bless you"—the appropriate response. But I was starting to fly once again so I laughed out loud, rolling from ecstatic awareness, reminded of the lucid line from the song Anna Begins, "Every time she sneezes, I believe it's love." I literally laughed out loud.

In retrospect, this made me appreciate John's earlier insight that things that made sense to me in this period seemed crazy to others. Anna Begins made sense to me—it symbolized new life. It definetly didn't make sense to others. Who the hell laughs when somebody sneezes? Only a mystic, I guess.

Mary grew more concerned not knowing what to make of my misplaced laughter. We definitely weren't in love, although we did care about each other, for whatever reasons on either side. Perhaps she saw a lot of light in me and cared about me extra because she knew something dark was starting to take over me. Perhaps I saw a lot of light in her too and cared about her extra because I knew she was slowly slipping to the dark side.

Regardless, "Stop it," Mary responded extra gently. "You're driving me crazy," she followed with the breath of a waning oracle.

I froze and vowed to keep quiet. This was the only time during the rave that I was absolutely speechless. Like Moses had power over sea, so this girl had power over me in this moment.

The realization that I was driving her crazy paralyzed me and made me realize that perhaps I was so far in outer space to know what was really going on in the concrete present. The smart girl that Mary was, she realized this and sung to my special state.

Her first time touching the music this trip, Mary softly and slowly put on the James Taylor classic "Fire and Rain".

"I like this song because it reminds me of my "*special friend*" she said emphasizing special and saying it devout and teary eyed as the opening acoustics started to soothe the atmosphere.

I knew this was Mary's secret way of communicating to me. She had remembered the story about the poetic rainstorm and was also aware of the Gospel Truth that I was a James Taylor soul based on our talks.

Mary's gentle gesture the source, my spirit was now at ease and my mood balanced, as I listened attentively to Mr. Taylor's authentic words.

Just yesterday morning they let me know you were gone (Morning after Manwhore Night?)
Susanne the plans they made put an end to you (Diaper Party?)
I walked out this morning and I wrote down this song
I just cant remember who to send it to

I've seen fire and I've seen rain
I've seen sunny days that I thought would never end
I've seen lonely times when I could not find a friend
But I always thought that Id see you again
Wont you look down upon me, jesus
You've got to help me make a stand
You've just got to see me through another day
My body's aching and my time is at hand
And I wont make it any other way

Oh, I've seen fire and I've seen rain
I've seen sunny days that I thought would never end
I've seen lonely times when I could not find a friend
But I always thought that Id see you again

The music illustrated Mary's care for me, instantly evoking a beautifully religious affection that I was very lucky to have a friend like her. The fact that she considered me her "special" friend drew the tears that I was trying to hold back from my sleepless and searching self. Despite this fact, however, Mark and I couldn't help but to argue with each other for the remainder of the ride.

"Mary, change this song, I want something I can get pumped up to, maybe a little Coldplay," he barked at her.

"Mark, stop being so fucking selfish all of the time. Maybe everybody else wants to listen to the song we're listening to. There are other people besides you." I snapped back.

"Alright Buddha." Mark quickly responded.

Mary could sense that she was an unspoken but main source of the burning tension between us. Rightfully, she grew frustrated with our classic, frat-boy style arguments.

"Boys, calm down, now!" She shouted.

"Ok, Mary." I responded dutifully.

"Dooshbag." Mark responded under his breath.

"Fuck you Mark!" I exclaimed.

"Boys!" Mary screamed.

"Chill out, guys. Mary was nice enough to give us a ride in her car. She's telling you to stop. And you're still arguing." John said in a Fatherly tone and was able to keep us silent until we pulled up to 39th street.

When we left her green Volvo, Mark gave Mary a hug and thanked her, but when I said thanks to Mary she didn't respond and quickly walked back into her house, frustrated by my overbearing presence.

"Oh man," I immediately thought to myself. "I'm in way too deep. I'm driving this poor girl crazy. I'm making my madness contagious."

I tried to play Ruit in my house but was so worried about the unspoken tension between Mary and me that I couldn't focus on my games and missed most of my shots.

"What's wrong, Castile?" My friends kept asking me. "You're always up for Ruit."

"Nothing." I replied very sad and lowly. I knew needed to talk to Mary, but believed that she didn't care to see me. She said I was driving her crazy. Still, I sensed that a dialogue must take place before it was too late—before summer ended and we just walked away indifferent and confused. She said I was driving her crazy but she also said I was a "sweet,

sweet man", her "special" friend, and saying goodbye to me moved her to tears. I was just really confused.

Freud said that the last stage of human development is the "psycho-sexual" stage—the stage where people learn and grow through physical intimacy. If Freud was right, and I really suspect he is right here, then that meant that I was underdeveloped to due my lack of intimate experience while my peers were fully developed due to their bounty of theirs. As a result, we didn't see the world with the same set of eyes. Through this insight I could make sense of my situation. Everyone around me was just more developed psychologically due to passing the final stage of human development. Not philosophically though. Herein lied the complexity and confusion this summer brought us all.

"Dude Castile, it's time for your haircut." John informed me after I lost in Ruit once again.

"C'mon man, I don't feel like getting one." I responded.

"Everyone else got a buzz when you were at your parents' condo last week. Are you with us or without us?" John followed.

Initially I was strongly opposed to the plan but then I remembered the expression, "When in Rome, do as the Romans do" so I accepted my fate.

"Alright man, let's do it." I said.

On my way downstairs to Jack's house, host of the electric razor, Mary—cognizant of our presence through her 1st floor Pink Palace window, stepped Biblically outside. She had something very important to say.

"I love Mark," she said affirmatively and followed with a hug. She meant love in the filial sense of course.

"I looooove John," she said more slowly and gave him an even bigger hug. Then she reached me. Our eyes locked.

"iiiiiiiiiiiiiiii" she said, trying whole heartedly to find the words but failing because of the unspeakable nature of what she was feeling, so I filled in the rest because I was feeling the same way.

Looking Mary in the eyes, speaking in the sincerest of all tones, I completed the puzzle, "Care about you way too much right now."

She quickly echoed my sincere words because they were so graceful, perfectly capturing the emotions we felt in our hidden depths. We did care about each other too much—so much we were driving each other crazy. For whatever reasons on either side. So much so that both of us would have interventions at the end of the summer courtesy of our friends. Mine would be for my grandiosity. Mary's would be for her alcohol abuse. Right now we were still kids too, so for the time, being "oracles", was a little too much for the both of us.

In this intimate moment however, our arms finally around each other, Mary said, "Chris I'll always be your best friend," and made the plea to preserve our special bond.

"No matter what?" I asked with the look of a puppy dog, evoking the possibility that she wouldn't be my best friend if circumstances change.

"No matter what!" Mary quickly exclaimed, confirming that she would be my best friend no matter what happened in the future. By doing so she instilled in me an inner peace so profound that it felt like God was with me playing aqueous transmission on his favorite angel's flute. Then John and Mark started to scream at me.

"C'mon Castile, let's go man. Get the fuck over here!" They wanted to cut my hair into a crew cut and they wanted it done now.

"You see why I need a girl best friend?" I asked Mary softly with a dose of humor and then walked over to John and Mark for what would be the most violent haircut of my life. Neither John nor Mark was a professional barber. Neither John nor Mark was sober.

I had finally submitted to the Way of the Pink Palace. Thus, the sovereign majority got their wish. Chris Castile was given a crew cut like everybody else, but not before forging a lifetime friendship with a girl that was unlike anyone else. Only the moons would know if living at the Pink Palace was the right choice but, no matter what, all were forgiven.

Crash

"The unexamined life is not worth living"—Socrates

Later that sticky August night, all forgiven yet the difference between wrong and right still crumbling, Mary and I reconciled but my head still spinning, I aspired to walk away from my ambivalent summer in Beach City.

When I walked outside my room around noon the next day to announce the good news, Mark was in the living room watching a porno entitled "Take it to the Limit".

"Sup boy?" Mark asked as I approached him.

"Sup Mark?" I replied.

"Um, hey, I think Mary would like this," he told me commenting on the porno.

"No she wouldn't." I snapped back as we gazed at the perverted imagery.

"Listen dude, I know something about Mary that you don't know. Something you'd only know if you hooked up with her." Mark replied.

"No, you don't." I said back at him hinting that I knew what he was talking about from educated guessing.

"All I am saying dude you gotta strike while the iron's hot." Mark responded.

"Well, that won't happen because I'm leaving today." I relayed back to him.

"Why do you want to leave man? We get fucked up everyday?" Mark inquired.

"Exactly" I said.

Inspired by an amateur desire to capture this signature moment—the final farewell of the Chris the Preacher, John grabbed his camera and trailed my motions.

"It was just my time, it was just my time," I said with a bittersweet smile on my way out the door, referencing American Pie with Counting Crows' "Walkways" blaring in the background.

"It was just my time." I said straight into the camera's recordable soul, immortalizing my last words.

Due to the fact that I was abandoning the chaotic lifestyle of Beach City, I felt a heightened sensed of placidity as I drove my mother's newly fixed car on the scenic route—Route 50, back to Bel Air. Still creatively colored at this moment in Time, I felt an intimate connection to nature as I cruised past the beautiful scenery that blessed my route home. The Chesapeake Bay, the childhood memory-evoking smell of the ocean on my way on out of the city, the gentle sound of the rain as I drove through the woods of Bel Air—these holy sensations gave me a more intimate communion with the Creator.

As I cruised home, inspired by my bucolic surroundings, I began to develop a key metaphor. Metaphorically, I was headed to the Garden of Eden—the mythical sanctuary where God lurked and metaphorically I was also leaving the heart of Ancient Rome—the raging inferno where faith was truly tested as God was far away. The driving thesis of the metaphor was that Home was where God most present for God is Love. And Ancient Rome where God was the most absent for Ancient Rome is Hate. I wasn't necessarily wrong in purely poetic sense.

In Beach City, there was no order, desires of the flesh were the only desires, and pretty much any behavior from threesomes to coke blowing to robbery were acceptable. At home, there was parental order, the affections of love rooted the time, and there were clear lines between acceptable and unacceptable behavior.

When I finally returned home, I did feel that special sense of God's presence, however, I still couldn't sleep. Therefore, I still couldn't feel a complete sense of homecoming. Something was keeping me up all night. I just didn't realize at the time what it really was.

The Pink Palace 2nd Floor. August 16, 2004.

"Where's Chris? I'm leaving for college tonight and wanted to say goodbye." Mary asked John, Peter, and Mark as she walked into the 2nd floor of the Palace and looked into Chris's room.

"Went home for the summer." John replied. "Said he was tired of this place. Too much sin he told me. He left you these though." John said as he handed Mary a bottle of pills.

"Oh my God. Oh Lord…These are his magic pills. He told me every time that he got sick his freshmen year of college he took them and was healed!" Mary said brightened.

"Well that's pretty cool he left those for you." John responded.

"Yeah, Chris is a great guy and when he does things like that it touches my heart, he just frustrates me sometimes. You know he didn't even say goodbye to me." Mary added.

"Yeah, I know what you mean. He keeps buttering you up, but won't make a move. For as brave as Chris is in some areas, he's pretty cowardly when it comes to girls." John answered.

"I know. He's too concerned with deep philosophical issues to just relax and kiss girls." Mary replied.

"I also think something is wrong with him medically. All of sudden, like near the middle of July, you know, he started to change. Like of all of sudden, he wasn't the kid I've known for the last twelve years. I think it might be some kind of defect in his brain. We've just been so fucked up all summer that we haven't really seen it clearly." Peter added.

"I don't know. It's like sometimes I feel like he's becoming like more religious. Like he's getting closer to God. Other times, I feel like no, he's just going crazy." Mark said.

"I think it's a little bit of both. You have to be a little cracked to see the light. Ta-ha." John interjected.

"I don't know what to think either." Mary said. "Here's this guy that is so sweet to me. That has so much creativity and insight, but still plays games with my heart. You know. Is he a genius? Does he something we all don't? Or is he just crazy? I don't

know. I was so crushed when I got dressed up for him and he didn't say one word to me. Not one fucking word. Then he gets all crazy when I hook-up with other guys. I don't know. I guess nobody's perfect and his heart is sincere, but he still has a lot to learn." Mary added.

"Yeah I could talk about Chris all day. My theory with him is that first of all, he's very smart. But that actually gets him in trouble. It's like he's too smart for his own good. His brain needs a lot of food to be full, that's why he's not content with just drinking and hooking up with chicks. Also, he was very religious as a little kid, so I think that explains why he's so religious now. He finally woke up after ignoring the call of God for so long. It was inevitable. But, too much religion can be bad for your health. God so mysterious and unknowable that if you try to understand him, like if he's always on your mind, then you'll start to go a little crazy. I think that's the case for Chris. Especially when you sex and drugs to the equation." John chimed in.

"Yeah, that's a pretty good assessment John." Peter responded.

"Well let's just pray that Chris gets better." Mary added. "I have to go now, it was wonderful meeting you guys. I have all of your screenames so we'll keep in touch."

"Bye Mary." Everyone responded.

"Good luck at Georgetown." John added.

The Castile Residence. Bel Air, MD. August 18, 2004.

After the third consecutive night home that I spent wide-awake had ended, I walked outside to admire the glory of the red, rising sun. Mindful of its natural symbolism, I realized that I had forgot to do something essential before I retired from the beach city life as I stared into the sun's ominous glow. I forgot to walk out to the "Gatsby Spot".

A small, Romantic dock overlooking the Chesapeake Bay, the Gatsby spot is where I first prayed after Mr. Paul died last summer. Since then, the Gatsby spot had become of significant sentimental value to me.

The Gatsby spot was a place of reflection, of prayer, and pretty much a sanctuary for the searching young adult soul. Last year, I went out there often to think and pray for my uncertain future.

This year though, I only went to the Gatsby spot a couple of times and in the beginning of the summer only. Thus, in my sleepless state of mind, where rationality only has a minor say, it was absolutely essential that I return to the Gatsby spot—no compromises. That's why I couldn't sleep as I saw it—I didn't go out to the Gatsby spot and say my prayers. Something was missing. I needed to make peace at that sacred place. The explanation for my insomnia was purely metaphysical.

So on an impulse; I drove back to the dunes on this hazy August morning despite surface rational sense. I didn't lie to my mother about my destination.

"Mom, I am going to McDonald's. I'll see you later." I told her.

However I omitted a crucial detail by not telling her that I meant McDonald's in Beach City. Of course my behavior was unusual, but it would inevitably be justified—the golden sun was an omen, an omen that pushed me toward an unforgettable journey.

On my important retreat from my home to 39th street's one and only mad house, I stopped at three different McDonald's. I ate breakfast at each one of them thereby securing one of the greatest glutton fests of my lifetime.

Successful in my mission of treating my taste buds to an equivalent to the jubilation that had been recently brewing in my brain, but now physically ill from consuming a year's worth of greasy sausage biscuits, I grew very lackadaisical during my drive to the dunes. I actually missed a critical turn. Fortunately though, despite the irregular beat of my McDonald's sponsored heart, I managed to correct the mistake and find the right path to Beach City.

As I approached the Pink Palace, three and a half hours after my departure from Bel Air, I saw John busting a fog on the porch. Long overdue for some comedy, I blared Sheryl Crow's "I wanna soak up the sun" just to see if he'd laugh of the site of his impulsive roommate blaring Sheryl Crow as he made his entrance to the Palace parking lot.

John laughed of course, and I greeted him with an athletic high five. Then I strolled into the house to wake up Mark.

"I love you dude, you're crazy as shit." Mark exclaimed upon seeing my surprising presence, "Take it to the Limit" on the TV screen.

From Mark's room, I called my mother and indicated my ironic whereabouts. "Mom, I'm near McDonald's…in Beach City." I informed her.

"Ummm, ok," she replied, very confused as to what to say.

Afterwards, I left the house with John to go yell at our realtors for giving us a noise violation fine. As I stepped boldly into Holiday Real Estate, the world's worse realtor's office, I immediately unleashed a comic diatribe.

"You guys are ridiculous. You could have told us that this house is tagged a "party house" by the cops every year. Or that our landlord is a complete sketch ball. But you wanted that ten grand so you kept quiet. Which leads me to say that we will rent from you guys…***Nevermore,***" and handed them our parking passes early in sophomoric style.

Inspired by our budding immaturity, John and I collectively conceived a brilliant idea—to eat buffalo chicken subs from Bellybuster's and then get tanked on the beach. Phase 1 of our perfect plan was to get the booze. None of us were 21 but I was packing…a Fake ID.

When we reached Lighthouse Liquors, I replaced my real license with my heat and now armed and dangerous—armed with an illegal government document and dangerous because I had a plan to use it, I walked boldly into the store. I routinely grabbed two cases of Rolling Rock bottles, and put them on the shelf like I belonged there. The fact that I was packing didn't matter because I didn't even get carded—I gave a strong performance as a confident 21 year old.

The old man behind the counter was a WWII veteran so I thanked him for his service, shook his hand firmly, and he then sold me two cases of Rolling Rock bottles without asking for proper identification. Stocked with booze and now hungry for Phase 2—Bellybuster's Buffalo Chicken, John and I drove southward to the immortal surfer shack.

On our way southward on Coastal highway to Buffalo Chicken heaven, John and I, both creative thinkers, started to brainstorm a film project—an investigatory documentary about a brilliant Social Justice teacher that was fired from Eckhart despite the collective will of the student body.

Mr. Gravy, the Social Justice teacher I speak of, was always critical of some of the hypocrisy certain faculty members demonstrated and wasn't asked back for a second term. Coincidence? We thought not.

In the thick of our burning conversation, John realized that we were now at a stoplight on 45th street—Bellybuster's home. The documentary, not my immediate surroundings buzzing in my head however, I walked out of his Honda Accord without looking for oncoming traffic.

On my brief walk to the median strip (Bellybuster's was Oceanside—our street bayside) I was suddenly numbed by a terrifying vision—a blue Bronco driven by an oblivious deliveryman coming full speed right at me.

"skkkkkkkkkkkkkkkerttt" was the last thing a heard before I turned my bone chilled body, thought crudely "Oh Shit", and then grinned and bore the piercing pain of getting absolutely hammered by an oncoming Blue Bronco.

As a result of getting drilled by this mass of piece of metal at 30 mph, I flew head over heels right on top of the median strip.

My head had been furiously flowing with creative ideation and then SMACK, cold objective reality incarnated in the form of a speeding Blue Bronco. Some have suggested that this was God's practical joke on me.

Yes, I was faithful. Yes, I was loving. Yes, most fundamentally I was humble. But I also, at times, due to my status as a serotonin-spun superman, was a complete jackass. I refused to hear the word "no", nor cooperate with any socially sovereign "authorities". I also felt like Teen Wolf because of the cocaine-like effect of the condition and like I was consequently, too cool for school.

Now, I'll always, even when balanced, never be afraid to challenge traditionally accepted worldviews and will still permanently hold a custom-designed picture of the world. However, I sometimes forgot, in my religious ecstasy, the critical fact that I wasn't God and therefore, to trust in the flow of the natural law rather than try to alter it. Thus, God being a practical joker, let me get hit by a car to pay for my pride. Or at least that's the Old Testament interpretation of the "accident".

As I lay wounded on the median strip, in a state of shock from the accident, I became fortunate enough to work up enough muscle to glance weakly in the direction of Bellybuster's. In my direct eyeline was a vision of religious dimension—the tattoos of a Vietnam veteran. The "aha" moment of insight achieved once again, I returned to my feet immediately despite my incessantly aching body.

I realized that the brave owner of the tattoos risked his life for America—I just got hit by a car. Relatively speaking, my situation was minute. Furthermore, I wanted to prove to this man that he didn't fight to preserve the freedom of a country of, in the words of Fred Locke (Mark's father), "Big babies." So inspired by the courage of a veteran as well as the wisdom of my best friends' firefighting Father, I returned to my feet a few short seconds after getting rocked by a Blue Bronco.

Two early teens, awestruck by the chain of extraordinary events approached me, "Wow, are you Ok dude? You need a cigarette?" they asked, a typically MTV-generated query.

"I'm ok, but I don't need a cigarette." I said as I pointed to my gold Florentine chain which symbolized my sincere faith in renaissance, or re-birth.

"Are you Jewish?" was their response. "Nope…I'm a soccer player, look it up" I told them just before I limped across 45th street to Bellybusters, serenaded by John's incessant laughter.

In a slow, painful, gimp I reached Bellybuster's, seemingly minutes later, and met the man that nearly ended my life—a white deliveryman dressed in Rastafarian attire.

"Dude, I'm so sorry. You're not going to sue are you?" The deliveryman inquired with a stoner's worry.

"No" I replied. "I'm not a scientologist."

"Well make sure they give you a beer," the deliveryman said high with relief.

"Ok, a beer will do." I replied as I sat down on a nearby bench satisfied that such a measure would instill the administration of justice.

Aching unbearably, I seated myself in concert with hearing a very familiar voice. "Dude, one second earlier and you'd be in trouble." Peter said.

"Don't you know your Torah, Peter?" I replied before verifying the presence of Peter's sun-glassed, shaggy haired self. "This was all part of Yahweh's master plan. It was my fate to get hit by a car and walk it off—I couldn't escape it."

"All I'm saying is you're lucky you didn't get seriously hurt." Peter replied medically.

Luck had nothing to do with it. This was God's Practical Joke. Instant Karma came to get me today, but not to signal the end of days. Rather,

Instant Karma came to get me in order to sober me up and bring me out of my romanticized dream trance.

I had lost touch with the hard reality of labor and pain ever since I quit work and started getting philosophical and poetic. Therefore, getting hit by a car wasn't an accident but rather a preordained, metaphorical, cold morning shower—God's way of waking me up from a heady, philosophical slumber by making me feel physical pain.

Regardless of the truth of such a claim, I did start to feel much tougher—much more like a 50's American man than I had been in the poetically pained past couple of weeks. As a result, my philosophical orientation shifted.

Nietzsche's bias was that philosophy had taken a wrong turn with Socrates who anointed Reason king. Before him the Greeks praised, above all others, ideals like courage, bravery, and strength.

After getting hit by a car while in the middle of a "creatively colored consciousness", feeling like Ray Lewis had just blindsided me, I rose like a Phoenix, with a revived conviction that Courage was the ultimate philosophical ideal. This is a conviction that I still hold true today despite rejecting all of Nietzsche's other ideas, especially the one about God—the reality of love that we all deify, somehow being dead.

Now hardened and sobered by a shocking accident, I joined Peter, Mark, and John for our ceremonial last buffalo chicken sub lunch as beach city bums. My first instinct was to cash in on my free beer, so I approached our waitress Mandy, confident that she would agree to the terms even though I was nineteen and therefore "underage" in loose legal terms.

I befriended her this summer and had a legit Fake ID. Moreover, my young life was nearly terminated by her restaurant's deliveryman and despite that fact I didn't plan to sue. My only request was very modest (and that's an understatement)—one cold National Bohemian beer in exchange for getting hit hard by their deliveryman's negligently speeding car.

"I'd like a National Bohemian, please." I told Mandy.

"I need to see your ID." She responded.

"You're kidding me right? Your employee almost killed me." But I had it, wasn't worried, and slyly handed her my "license".

"I'm from New Jersey, this is Fake. I can't serve you." Mandy said moments before I nearly started flipping over tables. I was old enough to go to war, I had been violently arrested and jailed this summer, her restaurant was responsible for nearly ending my life, and I couldn't even order a beer, from my "friend" with an ID that looked so real?

The brewing injustice made my blood boil like it was Ike Turner's crack-pipe and my head spin like it was Greg Focker's dreidel. I literally felt amidst one big episode of Seinfeld for my situation echoed that of a George Costanza. Thus, after I was denied the modestly proposed Natty Boh, I half-expected to hear the Seinfeld theme resonate from the Bellybuster speakers and Larry David to emerge from the woodwork and shake my hand on a great performance.

All my friends could say to comfort my emotionally and physically pained self was "She's just doing her job."

"Whatever" I responded in a broken tone, virtually speechless, just before downing my foot long buffalo chicken sub as soul food.

Following Phase 2, I walked back to 39th street just to prove my status as a hardass. When I reached the shores, I didn't say a word. I just sat in the sands and stared blankly at the great Ocean, Rolling Rock in hand, Phase 3 launched.

"What a summer," I thought to myself. "I think I've tred so much spiritual ground that I've dug too deep."

As I stared into the tasty waves with a cool buzz once again, I started to do some climatic reflection.

"Maybe life is simpler than I make it. Maybe all you have to do in life is to be a good person and do the best with the time that is given to you as Tolkien would argue. Look at those kids having a good time swimming in the ocean without a care in the world. Ignorant and in a state of bliss. That was me four summer's ago. Down the beach, playing sand soccer with my friends, without a care in the world. Maybe the Tao Te Ching is right on, "Throw away sacredness and wisdom and people will be 100 times happier." Ignorance is bliss. Maybe I'd be happier as a dumb slut who hooks up with a lot of girls and doesn't have the slightest clue about Plato and Aristotle then the reverse. And, in light of this fact, the philosophy of the Finchmeister is as valid as ever in the twenty first century world, "Love Life, Get Paid, and Get Laid."

The sun beat down on my crippled body, paralyzing the pained philosopher. All I wanted was to know the truth, was that so wrong? Maybe it was. Maybe I should have trusted in God's intelligent design and just worried about my own happiness and interpersonal ethics. I didn't realize this truth for years after this summer however.

"Maybe Woody Allen was right after all," I thought quietly, "when he said, "The unexamined life may not be worth living, but the examined life is no picnic either."

After about an hour of Oceanside reflection, I walked back into the Palace. When I did, John was there to greet me.

"Chris do you want to watch a video we made while you were gone?" He asked.

"Yeah that sounds cool." I replied as John pushed play on his new film which was pretty funny, but typical, consisting of the boys of summer partying during one of the nights I was sleepless in Bel Air.

John's latest work featured a Ruit tournament that ended, to my surprise (and I say that sarcastically), in complete chaos. The film concluded with John annihilating the Ruit table in a frenzy of random destruction and throwing a hammer through the window.

"Hammer" John shouted one second before tossing the hammer through the window. The spectacle may have seemed odd to the outside observer but not to me—it was just a typical night on the second floor of the Pink Palace.

The video run its course, my body still in excruciating pain, I took a hard-earned nap. I still planned to walk out to "The Gatsby Spot"—my initial destination, but when I woke I learned that Kevin Anselm was hosting a party at his house on 28th street. As a result, I decided to reserve my pilgrimage to the Gatsby Spot for tomorrow, making room for a recess from the hyper pious present. Celebration of youth the dominant idea and my Buddha belly full of delicious Buffalo Chicken, I marched to 28th street without the faintest idea that tonight would be easily the craziest night in the history of Christopher Castile.

Hope

"Hope is a waking dream"—Aristotle

We arrived at Anselm's beer bash earlier than most of the other neighborhood blackout stoners. Because we arrived early, the party was lame enough for us to leave it despite the three kegs stood proudly on Anselm, the pre-law student's, kitchen.

The amusement park Peter worked at featured an adrenaline injected ride—the Skycoaster so, without a fun fiesta to crash, we decided to peace roll there. Jack and his girlfriend Jenny, who had returned from a vacation in England, wanted to actually ride the Skycoaster. John and I just wanted a cure for our boredom. So off to the sky coaster we paraded like we were going down the yellow brick road. Dressed to party, I was wearing no shirt and a hat that said TOWN DRUNK.

Now I must assert, to clear the confusion, that despite what my attire may have indicated, I was still feeling like a symbol of the human search for Truth at this point in my life. I was seeing God in everything, undergoing intense conversion of spirit, and feeling fully invested into a more mystical reality. My heart felt like it was growing and I was fragile because of Mary. Therefore, the foundations were set for the deeply religious experience that inevitably unfolded.

Upon our posse's Skycoaster arrival, Peter, John, and I talked for a little while about life and the old neighborhood, nothing too deep, while Jack and Jenny rode the Skycoaster.

"We gotta get that One Way on Lancaster and Emerald changed when we get home. It's a crock of shit. Daniel got a ticket for going through it." I said to John and Peter just before I was interrupted by the sound of a loud, manly voice grounded in a Baltimore accent.

In search of the sound's source, I quickly turned around to see a stocky, Italian-American gentleman in an expensive suit. "You wanna meet the Governor?" The big man asked me.

Instantly, I looked left to see the awesome presence of Governor Robert Calvert. The timing was perfect—I was wearing no shirt, a hat that said Town Drunk, and yet felt prime for a serious discussion with my state's Governor. The scene was well worth a spot in a major motion picture.

As I stepped more closely to the Governor, I felt a piercing heart-sense that I was in the presence of an important human being.

"Who are you voting for in the election?" The Governor asked me with a hint of true curiosity.

I however, ignored his more political question and got deep with a more spiritual question. "Do you remember Paul Triumphant, governor?" I asked Calvert.

"I was sad to see him go." Governor Calvert instinctively responded in a tone of pure sincerity. Mr. Triumphant had made friends with Governor Calvert in the early 90's at NAMBLA and other sickness protests. From the protests, they became good friends. The Governor actually called the Triumphant house frequently and referred to himself as Bobby.

Mr. Paul even helped Bob Calvert become *Governor* Calvert by organizing a meeting of several African-American Baltimore City Pastors at his house. He cooked these pastors' delicious Italian dishes and let them hear Calvert's message. It must have worked because Governor Calvert was the first Republican to win Baltimore City in a gubernatorial race in over forty years.

In fact, Calvert thought so highly of Mr. Paul that Calvert told Mr. Paul that if he ever ran for President, he'd make Mr. Paul his advisor to religious affairs—an extremely important position especially in contemporary American politics. So the Governor truly was sad to see

Mr. Paul go—losing a good friend is hard, even if you are living the dream of governing your home state when he passes. Then the Gov repeated his original question.

"I mean my heart is with Rich, you know Compassionate Conservative, but unfortunately I'm going to have to vote for Donald Duck because the Electoral College picks the president—not the voter." I responded. The Governor laughed.

"Trust me, Paul is still with you," he quickly replied. Mr. Triumphant was always firm and unapologetic in his unique but authentic opinions.

"Why do you think kids your age don't vote?" The Italian man, Calvert's bodyguard followed by asking me.

I responded as if the result of careful practice, "I mean we're treated as inferior citizens. Why should we participate in a government that sends us to war, sentences us to jail, but doesn't even let us enjoy alcohol responsibly?"

"That's what I was telling him!" The Italian man sensationally said as he pointed to Governor Calvert. Then he asked me, "Are you in college?"

"Yes I am." I responded.

"Talk to me after college" the Italian man said as he walked away proud to have his political opinion seconded.

Before the Governor followed his bodyguard's step, he gave me the wisdom to "Think of Paul" at the polls in order to insure a legitimate vote for a real candidate.

"Wow! That was awesome! I just heard from the top political leader in the state the spirit of Mr. Paul Triumphant, a spirit of true conviction among many other positives was still with me," I thought, and I don't mean to be ironic, *triumphantly.*

The encounter confirmed my belief that this summer had been a very transformative one, rich in spiritual growth. It also confirmed my belief in the mystical nature of the afterlife. "Trust me, Paul is still with you," were my governor's carefully but confidently chosen words. Mr. Triumphant was still with a lot of people. His life was just that moving.

The odds of such a conversation with the Governor truly happening were so rare that it did made me wonder whether the concept of destiny really was more than just an ancient idea. It also made me wonder if the ominous sense to make a morning-lit drive to Beach City was something that cannot be reduced to pure delusion.

As I strolled back to Kevin's however, a lighter undertone of our conversation arose, "Holy Shit! I just told the Governor of Maryland that I was voting for Donald Duck for president while I was shirtless, sporting a hat that said, Town Drunk" I thought to myself. "And I got a job interview in spite of the fact."

What I said however, unusual as it may have been, still was true—the Electoral College did pick the president. The 2000 election, along with the US Constitution, is proof. Additionally, Maryland was a Democratic State and Philip D Liberal would win Maryland, no matter what.

The only reason why Calvert won the Democratic state of Maryland was because he was a true Marylander going up against a Massachusetts feminisita and had the support of other true Marylanders like Mr. Paul on his side. Rich didn't even bother to campaign in Maryland. Donald was the clear choice, my unique way of non-violently rebelling against an antiquated electoral system.

My encounter with my governor, as genuinely positive as it was, did have one negative consequence unfortunately. It made me feel invincible, like the law no longer applied to me due to the profound nature of our talk. I ended up getting burned by that consequence. No one, as I would soon discover, except a Republican under the Rich administration or Democrat in the oval office, is above American Law.

As our posse strolled back to 28th street, I thought it would be hilarious to moon Jack and Jenny—the super couple, so I followed through with my comedic instinct. I had forgiven Jack enough to go the Skycoaster with him, but couldn't help moon him and his girlfriend.

I was just being a kid, doing something kids do, having a good time, when suddenly a shout! The long of arm of the "Law" pervaded my religious reality once again. I turned around, bright eyed, to see a twenty year old, 110-pound cop with an angry look on his face.

"Hey, come here!" He said as if he was my master.

Turning back, I just laughed. "Are you serious dude? Leave me alone. I'm not harming anyone." I told the officer, completely frustrated at his point with Beach City police. I had good reason.

This whole summer, even before my Flight, was the story of a perpetual fight between my friends and the BCPD. Every one of my roommates, except me because I was in Bel Air during the bust, was arrested for making excessive noise. The cops always tried to bust our parties but only doing so successfully, and this is so ironic, on Independence Day by sending an undercover cop to probe our underage keg party.

I had Fake ID's taken from me, warrants out for my banishment from the property (legal technicality in the beginning of the summer. I hadn't signed in at the realtors therefore was not allowed on the premises), and was blindly harassed many times walking home from McDonalds. Naturally, "Beach City Police suck dick" was our team motto. So when this cop got in my face after I was just home for the summer, I lost my patience and decided to not to tolerate any more nonsense.

"You just mooned that car," he replied.

"No I didn't." I countered truthfully.

"I'm going to have to ask you some questions." Officer Hatey snapped back.

"Buddy, I really don't feel like dealing with this right now. Either charge me with something or let me go." I told the young officer.

He instantly became furious, demanding "Don't get an attitude with *me*."

From just forty seconds of dealing with him I identified his type. He was one of those scrawny kids who got picked on when he was little and wanted to join the police force to take out his bottled up anger on others. Unlike police in most other areas, generally brave, reasonable, and policemen in the name of civil service, he was a policeman in the name of power because he was the kid that everybody made fun of for being a loser. Thus, now backed by the badge, Hatey had a legal vendetta against fun, unapologetic in his use of police force to investigate 12:30 a.m. three second August Mooning.

The scene, despite the surface seriousness—criminal vs. cop, was actually very comical. The scene essentially featured a shirtless revolutionary and uniformed conservative exchanging words in the party block of a family-oriented beach resort.

"You're not going anywhere until I get some answers! What's your name?" Officer Hatey demanded.

"I don't have to tell you shit. Just leave me alone! I'm not doing anything "morally" wrong. I'm not stealing, fighting, or putting anyone's life in jeopardy. I just showed my bare ass off. Adam and Eve the archetypical humans were kicked out of the Garden, not for being naked, but for being embarrassed to be Naked! I'm not embarrassed to be naked. I mooned my friend, big deal. Aren't there such a thing as crimes?" I squawked at the stranger.

Hatey grew angrier and called his superior via Walk-E-Talkie. "Yeah, we've got a teenager who just mooned a car. Can I arrest him?"

"No, it's not an arrestable offense." Hatey's superior said through the Walk-E-Talkie.

I overheard the supervisor's speech and gave a smile. "Good Night," I told Hatey.

"Wait a minute! I still can perform a GVD and extract some information," Hatey replied desperately.

"Listen man. Listen up. I've been awake for two straight days. Two straight days and I'm fucking tired not to mention I got hit by a god damn car today. You can't arrest me for my actions. Not even close. So you need to let me go now." I said.

"What's your name??!!" Hatey screamed for the third time.

"Ugh, just make this quick." I said, finally cooperative. I now sensed that answering this butt pirate's stupid series of unnecessary questions would be the only way to drive him away from Power Trip land. I was impulsively compliant. If I was being rational, I would have realized that there was nothing that he could really do to me. But I wasn't and didn't have much knowledge of public law either, so I gave Hatey my legal name—Thomas Christopher Castile (yes my first name was Thomas but I went by Christopher because my Catholic grade school teachers always called me Doubting Thomas despite my sincere faith).When he asked for my address however, I hesitated.

I didn't want my parents to find out about this incident because it wasn't an act of conscientious objection, but rather crude immaturity. So

I said, "Well I have three addresses. The Pink House, Sacred Heart College, and Bel Air."

"Listen up. Don't get smart with me. What's your address?" Hatey snapped.

"No you listen up, God's my authority not some scrawny ass meter maid." I rebutted.

"What are you some stupid high schooler?" Hatey responded, unknowingly setting himself up for a verbal assault of philosophical musings.

"No, I'm a college student who happens to be a lot smarter than you." I immediately answered. This comment drove Hatey to the brink of absolute frustration.

People usually blindly cooperated with police. Not me, at least with Beach City Police. They were such bad police that even other police ripped on them. The cop that arrested me at Merryweather said, "Beach City Police *are* dooshbags man." They make a living busting legal adults for drinking alcohol and then expect people to respect their civil service.

If Hatey would have shown one thread of bravery or wisdom, not have immediately adopted a "holier than thou" hardass mentality upon witnessing my August mooning, or simply not have been a Beach City Police officer, I would have given him my respect. But this guy was the antithesis of a real cop—stationed in Beach City, treating a bare ass like an armed robbery, and completely condescending.

"Do you have any pending trials or court dates?" Hatey furiously followed staying faithful to the GVD code of conduct.

"Um well, actually I have a trial for interrupting some Howard County cops while they wrote alcohol citations." I answered with laughter.

"Oh, so you hate cops." Hatey impulsively concluded.

"No, I hate *Beach City* cops because of bullshit like this. I mooned my friend for three seconds and you're acting like I just robbed an orphanage. What do you think a just God would think of your treatment of me?" I asked the rookie officer, evoking a heavy metaphysical proposition uncharacteristic of a mere "stupid high schooler".

"I don't think you know what you're talking about." Hatey stuttered with serious, scared, shakes in his tone.

"In matters of God and justice, I think I absolutely know what I am talking about. I'm a philosophy major at Sacred Heart College, I've been going to Catholic mass since I was a child, and know that the Golden Rule is the most important rule to follow."

"Give me your address you stupid teenager!" Hatey screamed like he probably did during gym class.

Sensing this whole ordeal was evolving into a divine comedy of errors and misunderstanding, I turned to the only tactic I knew—civil disobedience. My primal senses urged me to jack him in the face, but I didn't want to take the anthropomorphic route and do that, so I just took the educated route and stopping playing his game through Thoreau's political resistance tool. Some may say this behavior was eccentric, and they are probably right, but later when I told this story to my professor—an ordained minister in the United Church of Christ with a master's in divinity from Yale aged eighty years, he was quickly inspired to give me a heartfelt blessing.

"You know what, I'm going to take the position of the Great Gandhi with a non-violent approach to this situation." I said and lied down on the grass, marveling at the silent stillness of the starts. I finally felt like I was free from the rule of unnecessary law as I was behaving peacefully, in harmony with the Tao as I imitated the 20th century's most famous pacifist.

"Get up!" Hatey screamed.

I just tuned him out. In fact, I tuned out the entire material world and was completely content just, to use a hippied-out term "being".

"What a marvelous night." I thought, despite being harassed by a cop in the present. "Trust me Paul is still with you," were the immortal words of Governor Calvert.

"I had a heart to heart with my state's governor." I thought to myself as I communed with the angels in heaven, reflecting on the life of a faithful departed.

Covered in Rain

I was on Senior Week, walking into a party at Grace's house when I saw two of my friends standing still with the saddest looks on their faces.

"What's wrong, guys?" I asked them.

"Mr. Paul died," they responded so saddened they could barely speak it.

"No you're joking." I said to them, unable to accept the news at first. I knew Mr. Paul was in the hospital but didn't know that it was that serious.

"Chris, we wouldn't joke about something like this," they said back to me.

I took a pregnant pause and looked at the funeral sober expressions on their faces. When the piercing reality of Mr. Paul's biological death finally hit me, I instantly burst into a frenzy of tears.

I kept crying and crying, saying nothing, never opening my eyes, until I found myself upstairs in a bedroom along side Grace, Julia, and one other young lady…Elizabeth.

"Oh yeah, I remember now." I thought to myself, the last fifteen months somewhat blackouted of my memory. "Elizabeth came to Senior Week from California. And she was there by my side when Mr. Triumphant died. That was the last time I saw her. I walked home with John, Mark and Peter, put on DMB's Before These Crowded Streets and cried myself to sleep…maybe I should have stayed with Elizabeth. Maybe we could have talked right there, I could have cried in her arms, and then eased into the intimacy that Mr. Paul knew he were destined for. He said, "Don't lose her". Everything that came from his mouth was the product of a careful wisdom. Therefore he had to have seen something special in us being together.

Oh Lord, I wish I could go back. Things would have been different. I would have had the experience of my first healthy, intimate relationship. I wouldn't have needed to care about philosophy and religion because I'd have a treasure beyond price—a beautiful woman, in my appreciative arms. If only I had forgiven Elizabeth when I should have…"

In this concentrated, philosophical meditation I was interrupted, not by the pleas of Hatey (which I faded out), but rather by the docile but thoroughly unexpected sound of stroller. I looked up to see a woman was pushing a child on a stroller around me at 12:45 a.m. in the middle of one of the city's worst neighborhoods.

"That's it, that's it!" Hatey exclaimed. "I can arrest you now! You didn't allow the free passage of another citizen in public!" He followed as I looked at him in a human decency inspired shock.

I could get arrested, fingerprinted, mug-shotted, sent to jail, and summoned to court for further punishment *literally* because some lady pushing a kid in a stroller in one of the city's worse areas had to take three whole steps around me! It was sickening to see the joy that overwhelmed him as he realized that he could arrest me. This man was obviously seriously ill, heavily intoxicated with state granted power.

"Get up, you're going to jail!" Hatey cheered like he had somehow "won" this bizarre game.

Once again, I had fought the law, and the law emerged victorious, at least in a loose legal sense—definitely not in a moral sense though. Hatey actually celebrated the fact that he could arrest me—typical BCPD. As the iron handcuffs were placed on me, the BCPD cruiser arriving to ship me to jail, I just shook my head in disappointment.

"This is messed up dude. They give this guy a gun and legal authority by passing a two-week training course. BCPD suck dick."

On the car ride to jail, my mind ran in eight different directions. But despite the unfortunate situation, my optimism never ceased. Handcuffed in the back of a police car, I dreamed tie-died abstractions about the meaning of forgiveness. How ironic the situation was—a two time criminal with a conscience pondering philosophical abstractions in the back of a police car, bleeding on the back seat.

As we neared the Big House, I replayed my encounter with the Governor in my head, and recognized his wisdom as priceless and the story of my conversation with him—a local legend to be passed on for generations. "Trust me Paul is still with you." I thought to myself as I arrived to jail for the second time this summer. This was a highly inconvenient experience once again.

I had been awake for nearly forty one hours when I arrived. I was arrested only because a lady had to walk around me on the street. I had been hit by a car earlier in the day and still felt an unbearable sting on my lower body. And taking someone's freedom, when unmerited, is Anti-American.

A real danger to society with my oversized conscience, I had my fingers printed, mug shots taken and then was tucked neatly in an individual jail cell. Now enraged against the machine, I rambunctiously rebelled in my iron cell despite Big Brother's cameras. I had no remorse, however—the Beach City Police had arrested an innocent man with a plan to practice the golden rule.

I decorated the room with toilet paper and yelled out obscenities for a short span until I realized they were falling on deaf ears. In search of some sleep, I did almost fifteen push-ups before I climbed into my ghostly, white cot and quickly passed out due to my lack of physical fitness.

In the thick of a lucid dream about my wonderful parent's and my Eckhart days—the glory days when I could actually sleep every night and laughed non-stop everyday, a loud voice crept into my subconscious causing an abrupt end to my homeward bound dream.

"Ok man, you can go now." The voice reported.

I rose in one of those semi-conscious, brilliant moments, between dreaming and waking up to see a young police officer at my cell. Dutifully, he handed me my report, signed me out, returned my possessions—gold chain and Eckhart ring, and sent me on my way home.

That marathon night, the moons glowing in cosmic triumph, I limped shirtless with a Florentine chain around my neck and "Town Drunk" hat on my head, for over one hundred streets (almost eight miles)—141st to 39th, in completion of the great trek home. It was a noble battle fought alone and in pain, thus symbolizing my young adult life. But like the young adult life it symbolized, my trek had a driving constant—Hope.

In its own case, the hope was that I'd inevitably reach my big comfortable bed where I'd earn a dream slumber. In the case of my young life—it was the metaphysical Hope that one day I'd find a peaceful resolutions to my deep questions and sleep thereafter alongside my queen. It's a hope that I'll never abandon.

* * *

I woke up a free man, liberated from the chains and shackles of the modern machine. The warm August sun radiating throughout the beach house as a result never felt so glorious. The morning view of the beach through my window was a gift of freedom, perhaps the most sacred on the planet.

In a celebratory hymn as I rose from bed, the immortal words of Roger Waters flowed through my consciousness, "breathe, breathe in the Air don't be afraid to care" as weeks of devout search culminated into this moment—calm, soothing, natural, the Shinto reality. The sun in all of its Glory still rose as it had since the beginning despite my sneaking suspicion that it would do otherwise. August 19 was a new day, a fresh start, and a blessing that I thoroughly appreciated.

I spent it in recovery sprawled out on the sands, simplifying my answer to the question of everyday ethics. "Live by the sun, love by the moon, and stay faithful to the Golden Rule. What more could we ask?" I thought feeling as if I had solved, after years of hard work, some intricate ethical equation.

After this long day religion and spirituality jam session had waned, I limped back to my house for a catnap because the hot August sun had drained my energy. When I woke from a rare slumber it was night—ideal time to return to the Gatsby spot, and make a covenant with the Author of Creation. I decided that this would be my last night in Beach City so knew that I had to spend it in peace, free from government captivity. So off to the Gatsby spot I quietly drove to on this still August Night well under the 40 MPH speed limit.

As I cruised down Coastal Highway I couldn't help but wonder what Mary Cooper was doing. I knew that she was now engaged on the life-changing college experience in the suburbs of Washington, DC, but still had deep, heartfelt questions.

"What would our futures be like? Would we always be friends? Would she ever meet my parents? Would I meet hers? Would she ever come to visit me at Sacred Heart? Would I ever visit her at Georgetown? Or would we just forget the sparks we saw and grow indifferent to each other? Or would we, since we only knew each other for three months, only two of which I was healthy, not have enough mutual experiences to ground the friendship?

Would she just write me off as crazy and never talk to me? Would she make enough guy friends that she wouldn't feel the need to have me in her life? Would we just go off astronomically in our own, separate directions and never reunite? Or we would we care about each other's unique lives enough to drop the occasional phone call or letter? Would we make a commitment to stay faithful to that late summer's eve promise to be best friends no matter what or would we write that promise off as a stamp of a confusing time and rarely talk?" I contemplated very curiously.

When I finally reached the 7th street dock, the bright lights in the distance instantly began to illuminate my senses. They represented my future, or so I hoped—very evocative.

I sat at the dock's edge, which symbolized the period of my life that I was fully bound to—the edge of my childhood, a sometimes confusing and ambivalent but generally speaking, exciting time grounded in hugs and humor. Just ahead were the dark waters of the Chesapeake Bay—early adulthood, the Great Unknown. I would immerse myself in those murky waters soon, but for now, I just reached out into the distance like Gatsby reaching out for the green light and said a prayer for a safe journey.

That's all I could really do. I wasn't an oracle, I wasn't a prophet, and I couldn't tell the future. I now knew, thanks to my humbling arrest and recent conversion-like experiences, how small I was in the grand spectrum of the universe. And so I just put my faith in the conception that the Grace of God would guide me through life's perennial mysteries as I said my final goodbye to a rocket summer in Beach City, MD.

Gravity

"Faithless is he that says farewell when the road darkens" -Tolkien

"Hi, Mrs. Teresa, it's Peter." Peter announced over his flip phone.

"Oh hi, Peter. How are you?" Mrs. Castile responded from her home.

"I'm doing pretty well, but I'm worried about Chris." Peter followed.

"He's not the same. Something is wrong with him. He got arrested last night. He laid down in the street imitating Gandhi." Peter continued.

"Oh dear. Is he ok?" Mrs. Castile responded.

Well, he's not in jail anymore, but I'm not sure if he's ok mentally. He's just being doing some bizarre stuff all summer. I think it might be an imbalance in his brain. We've been thinking about calling you and Mr. James for the past four weeks but didn't because we didn't want to betray Chris. But this is too much. We want our best friend back." Peter said slightly teary eyed.

"Oh Lord. I know how you feel. We want our son back. I can't stand to see him suffer like this but Chris is so opinioned you know, so fixed in his beliefs, that it'll be hard to get through to him. You know?" Mrs. Castile answered.

"Oh, Ms. Teresa, we've realized that. But still, I thought we should let you know that it's getting pretty bad. You're not here to see it." Peter informed Mrs. Castile.

"Thanks Peter. Chris is really lucky to have friends like you and I'm so glad you're telling me this. I think James and I are going to make an appointment for him to get checked out. But I'd like to do it soon, so he doesn't do more bizarre stuff at school." Mrs. Castile followed.

"Yeah it's just a difficult situation. Sometimes your son is brilliant, other times he makes us worry. In the state he's in now though, we can't make him realize the latter. He won't listen to us." Peter told Mrs. Castile.

"I couldn't agree more. We're going to schedule an appointment with a therapist soon, so hopefully he can get through to him." Mrs. Castile said.

"I hope." Peter concluded.

I strolled into the Pink Palace high off my Gatsby inspired musings where I saw a circle of concerned stares.

"Chris, we need to talk to you." Peter informed me.

"No you don't, you guys don't understand. You don't know what it's like to be me. I'm seeing the Truth. At some point in your lives you'll see it too."

"Chris, do you know how arrogant that sounds?" Mark objected.

"It's not arrogant, dude. Fuck that. I'm optimistic that you'll discover Truth sometime. You just have to sober up a little bit." I followed.

"Alright, but Chris—you got arrested last night. You got arrested at Merryweather. You drove Mary crazy. Is that Truth?" Mark asked.

"Fuck that dude. Don't bring Mary into this. I didn't drive her crazy. And yes, that is Truth. Jesus got arrested. Gandhi got arrested. Socrates got arrested. Getting arrested unjustly is a highly religious experience." I answered.

"But Chris, you're not Socrates. And you didn't get arrested unjustly—you broke the law. Oh, and if you didn't drive Mary crazy then why did she say, "Stop it, you're driving me crazy" in the car when we went to Wendy's then?" Mark objected.

"You don't know Mary like I do." I responded.

"Well I have seen her naked. She did let me play with her snatch." Mark said with a chuckle.

"Fuck that shit. Fuck you Mark. I'm tired of this summer. I'm tired of all of this sex bullshit. I'm tired of everybody trying to preach to me. Let me be. I'm on a journey and you assholes can't stop me. Screw you guys, I'm going home." I asserted.

"Chris, wait dude. Don't listen to Mark. All I'm saying is that you're making your parents worry that's all. You need a little help. We all love and want what's best for you dude." Peter pleaded.

"Well what's best for me is to leave this sinful place behind. Peace." I vowed.

The ride home was spent in complete contemplation. Three hours of devout thought. When I walked into my house it was in complete silence. I barely said anything to my parents for the next few days. I turned off my cell phone so my friends couldn't call me. There were some real dark nights of the soul to follow, to use a term from F Scott Fitzgerald. I stayed in my room reading Lord of the Rings and thinking for the majority of the time.

* * *

Three days had passed until I was brightened. I was surfing the internet in a deep silence when I noticed an internet advertisement on the Eckhart website.

August 23, 2004. 40th anniversary celebration. All alumni welcome. Free Food and Drinks. 6:30-9:00 p.m.

I thought that returning to my *alma mater* would instill within the therapeutic sense of homecoming that I needed. I really missed that place. Going to school there was easily the greatest four years of my life. I didn't even feel like going back to Sacred Heart. So on August 23rd at 6:15 p.m. I left my house for the first time in three days. I was now in an amplified mood fresh off a thorough reading of the Lord of the Rings trilogy.

When I reached the heart of the sleepy town, I performed a wacky life science experiment based on my theory that the residents of Bel Air, in general, were pretty sketch.

For artistic purposes, I wanted to see what would happen if I threw a copy of the green "High times" magazine—a counter-cultural symbol, on the grass of McDonald's at the heart of Bel Air. My thesis was that one of the townspeople would react negatively to my artistic act of littering, act "holier than thou" judgmentally, and therefore validate my theory that the residents of Bel Air, in general, were sketch. My thesis proved unwavering true and actually went to a level of extremity that I didn't expect despite being in Harford County.

Immediately after throwing a copy of *High Times* on the grass, I looked to the right lane to see an angry fat woman.

"Hey" she yelled. "You can't do that," pointing to me, coinciding universal morality with adherence to the local law.

I just shrugged, put a Ronald Reagan tribute magazine on my roof and, in a random act of improvisation, drove toward my Catholic destination unable to prevent myself from bursting into uncontrollable laughter.

"Bel Airians are so predictable." I said out loud to myself as I neared The Meister Eckhart School.

This woman was legitimately enraged. I guess littering was a mortal sin in her "I am going to save the world and feel good about myself by bringing an artistic polluter to justice" schema.

As we parted ways on the road, she made sure that I saw her authoritative signal that she would call the Harford County Police on my poetically polluting self. First, she flicked me off and then she pointed to her phone threatfully.

I was not scared because I'd butted heads with law enforcement plenty of times in the near past. Furthermore, at this point in my life, I was still searching for Truth, refusing to let threat of petty legal punishment deter me in that pursuit. Additionally, I had adopted the one of the most practical and important of all Christian teachings—"Perfect love casts out fear". My perfect love of Truth, Justice, and Beauty casts out my fear of sketchy Belairians calling the police on me for littering.

"James, where's Christopher?" Mrs. Castile asked her husband over the house phone.

"I dunno. Did you call his friends?" Mr. Castile inquired.

"They said they haven't seen or heard from him in a few days." Mrs. Castile responded.

"Did you check his room? He's been in there for the past few days." Mr. Castile answered.

"Of course I checked his room. I called his cell phone to and it went straight to the answering machine. He hasn't been feeling very good so Lord knows what he's doing. Honey, I'm worried. He didn't leave a note or anything. Maybe he's having another episode." Mrs. Castile replied with great worry. "Why don't we call the cops to see if they can track down his tags?" She followed.

"Well let's wait to see if he comes home tonight or calls us." Mr. Castile said back.

"But James, that might be too late." Mrs. Castile pleaded to her husband.

"Stop worrying. Our Son's fine." Mr. Castile concluded.

"Better safe then sorry. I'm calling the cops to see if they can find him." Mrs. Castile concluded.

I reached my alma mater three minutes after my brief altercation with the righteous townie and quickly eased into a happy state after I entered the place where I had made some of my most treasured memories. Being at Eckhart just soothed my aching soul with a warm sense of home, especially when I got a chance to talk as an adult with some former teachers.

"Hey, Mrs. Garfield." I said to Mrs. Garfield John's mom—Eckhart field hockey coach and health teacher. "A summer in Beach City will really make you grow up fast. How's John?"

"Christopher Castile," John's mother replied. "I thought I'd see you here. John's doing well but he's back at school now. He says that he has a great idea for a movie."

"I think I have an idea of what it's about." I responded just before I started to wander through the perfect brown building. In the gym I noticed some current students setting up for the next day's homecoming dance. Inspired by the nostalgic sight of my high school self in some of these kids, I decided to try to do a good deed by walking out to my car and bringing in some Dave Matthew's CD's for them to listen to.

"Harford County Police." Officer Hume answered from his Bel Air office.

"Yeah. Hello Officer. I was wondering if you could find my car for me. My son is driving it and we're pretty sure he has a mental disorder that is unmedicated. He doesn't have his cell phone on, he hasn't called us, he didn't leave a note, and we're very worried about him." Mrs. Castile responded.

"Yeah I can do that for you. I have kids myself, one of them has severe ADHD. I understand. What's the tag number?" Officer Hume followed.

"303 BOE" Mrs. Castile answered.

"What's the mold and year?" Officer Hume inquired.

"It's a 91' Pink Cadillac." Mrs. Castile replied.

"Ok. We'll alert the officers to be on the lookout for your vehicle and hopefully your son too. Can I contact you at this number?" Officer Hume asked.

"Yes. Thanks officer, God Bless You." Mrs. Castile told Officer Hume.

As I strolled out to my car to grab the disks, I was just so far into Plato's form world at this point in my life—so far away objective reality, that I left my car doors open. Not unlocked, but literally open. Such was absentmindedness at its best. My head was so heavily endowed with astronomical abstractions about the existence of eternal realities, cosmic craftsmanship, the meaning of life, that I could not focus, even minutely, upon the world that was right before my eyes. At least when I wasn't around people.

I returned to the forty year old building, dropped off "Dave Matthews and Tim Reynolds: Live at Luther College", and began, once again, to chat enthusiastically with some alumni and teachers, oblivious to the reality of my opened car doors. Noticing my young adult presence, Mr. O' Malley—the school's principal, told me "Just to clarify, I'm glad that you're here," (I had some disciplinary issues at Eckhart. Not too much of a surprise. I was a good kid at heart, but a class clown none the less. On one controversial occasion I was banned from the Senior Variety and nearly kicked out of school, largely due to Mr. O'Malley's "zero tolerance" alcohol policy) and we began to talk about Eckhart athletics—a common interest.

"The soccer team is sure missing you guys." Mr. O'Malley informed me.

"Yeah they sure are. We had quite a crew." I responded.

In the thick of our sporty discussion, the women that had been angered by my act of creative, counter-cultural pollution suddenly emerged out of the darkness! The door to the function was open and approachable to people approaching from outdoors, maybe it should not have been for exactly this reason.

"Not what I expected," she said in a detective tone before flying away in the sticky bucolic night in her oversized Baltimore Ravens shirt.

"Nevermore." I sternly said back to her.

Only minutes later, the woman returned in a flustered mood furiously shouting "Teresa Castile! Teresa Castile!" the name of my mother. Now, I knew exactly what she was thinking because, despite my unfortunate condition, I was still a pretty bright guy.

I knew that this lady wanted to bust me for littering, but when she saw me at Eckhart—a respected institution in the community, she curbed her appetite for bringing random artistic polluters to justice. However, she still wanted to see who I was. Therefore, she called the cops and got the name of the owner of the car I was driving which she expected to be me. But it wasn't. The car was registered in the name of Teresa Castile—my mother. So when my concerned fellow Bel Airian discovered that I most likely was not named Teresa Castile due to my masculine features, she automatically jumped to a striking conclusion. Her conclusion was not the simple conclusion that Teresa Castile may have been the name of a *family member* but rather the real conclusion as she saw—it was the name of the unfortunate women who's car I had stolen right before I went on a littering spree in the heart of Bel Air.

And so I let her continue frantically shouting, "Teresa Castile, Teresa Castile," in her oversized Ravens T-Shirt just to make her believe for a hot second that she had solved some intricate grand theft auto crime. Finally though, I retaliated by saying, "Teresa Castile is my mother, you freakin' sketch artist. Now, go mind your own goddamn business!" and finally put an end to this sweet symphony of nonsense.

Knock out stunned, she returned to her purpose driven life quickly after my piercing words, never to forget that one special moment where she nearly snagged a high-profile criminal. But the dramatic series of events would not end there. My absent minded act of leaving my mom's car doors open on private property yielded amazing results.

"Mr. O'Malley a police officer is here to talk to you. Could you come outside please?" An alumnus said.

"Sure" Mr. O'Malley responded.

"Mr. O'Malley. I'm Officer Di Livio from the Harford County Police. There's a vehicle parked on your property with open doors. The owner of this vehicle is named Teresa Castile. Name sound familiar?" Officer Di Livio asked.

"Yes. She's the mother of one of my former students. Her son Chris is actually at our alumni function." Mr. O'Malley answered.

"Oh, do you know why his car doors are opened?" Officer Di Livio followed.

'I don't know." Mr. O'Malley replied.

"You think an angry girlfriend did it?" Officer Di Livio inquired.

"Perhaps. Although you never know with Chris Castile. He's quite an interesting character. He never ceases to amaze. He could very well be playing a game with us." Mr. O'Malley answered.

"Yeah. His mother did tell us that he might have a mental disorder." Officer Di Livio responded.

"Well I can retrieve him so we can discuss this matter and find out what really happened." Mr. O'Malley asserted.

Seven minutes after the Bel Airian in an oversized Ravens shirt vanished, Mr. O' Malley came inside the building very urgent in his demeanor.

"Chris you have got to come outside, the cops are looking for you. It looks as though someone has broken into your car!" Mr. O'Malley announced.

"Oh man, this ought to be interesting," was my instant reaction when I nervously walked outside to see a conscientious cop at the car's side.

The cop saw the disarray that the car was in and speculated that an angry girlfriend had broken into my car, messed up the inside, opened the doors, and drove off grinning in the pale moonlight.

"I haven't had a girlfriend in nearly three years," I responded. "And she lives in California," assuring him that no such activity had occurred. Then I just improvised some two-cent answer to calm everyone's queries and instill a comedic end to the entire situation.

Too embarrassed to concede that I was so far into outer space to notice that I had left my car doors open, I called on my comedic instincts to save me, "I just wanted to show Mr. O' Malley here that I trust my belongings when they're at Eckhart because I have faith in my alma mater." I said like I was uttering the closing lines in a sitcom.

The cop quickly burst into laughter. He was a nice Italian man and I respected him because he actually took the time to listen rather than simply dictate.

"Wait till the boys at the force hear about this one." Officer Di Livio said to us and drove off in the silent Bel Air sky.

I tried to walk back inside after inserting a happy ending to my story, but Mr. O' Malley stopped me.

"Let's have a talk, Chris," he said.

Then Mr. O'Malley called my Father and told him to pick me up at Eckhart cognizant of the reality that I was too far in the form world to safely operate a motor vehicle.

Despite my absent mindedness, our conversation was as deeply intellectual a conversation as I've ever had. Mr. O' Malley had a stigma around my group of friends and their parents as "bad guy" but I generally liked him. He was just misunderstood.

A brilliant linguist with a genuine faith, very mature philosophically and well-educated, Mr. O'Malley made a fine principal. His main flaw, and this was the source of the majority of the distaste for him the Eckhart community held, was his lack of connection to the culture his students were coming from. He didn't realize that there was no way to keep teenagers in America from boozing and doing drugs, despite being baptized Catholic. Furthermore, he expected that the average student would rally against booze and drugs even to go so far as to Narc on each other—an ideal simply out of sync with the twenty first century American reality. We all had learned, courtesy of Goodfellas, the two most important lessons in life, "Never rat on your friends and always keep your mouth shut."

That controversial topic spared from our discussion however, we spoke using cleverly chosen language, and instead talked about more important issues like literature, people, and the Bible. "Well in the Kingdom of God, I guess we have room for one or two eccentrics." Mr. O'Malley informed me.

I took this judgment as a blessing, but I still thought it was slightly inaccurate. Mr. O'Malley didn't understand me completely because he had a permanent home in Irish Catholicism. He never stepped outside himself to examine himself in Kantian fashion as I did. However, I was keenly aware of the immortal words of the Transcendentalists, "To be Great is to be misunderstood" and that's why I didn't take issue with Mr.

O' Malley's slight misunderstanding. Especially because it was based on a temporary version of myself.

To illustrate the legitimacy of my young adult growth in spirit and show that I was more than just a simple eccentric, I mentioned JRR Tolkien and the Christian symbolism of his works.

"JRR Tolkien's literature is well versed in the Bible." Mr. O'Malley told me just before I countered by saying "Return of the King. I got it." (Return of the King=Return of the Messiah. LOTR starts with the missionaries leaving The Shire—Home, similar to the Garden of Eden and ends with a return to The Shire but only through the saving grace of the messianic king.)

Then we talked briefly about my favorite book—The Great Gatsby and he commented, "Perhaps you've found something that you're willing to go all-in for and risk everything to preserve," fully capturing the true love or nothing essence of the story.

"Hopefully one day, you can meet my Daisy." I told Mr. O'Malley, optimistic that I would find my queen one day.

Our literary discussion evolved to the very controversial subject of censorship. The books I spoke of—Lord of the Rings, Catcher in the Rye, The Bible were among the most banned books in American schools. Mr. O' Malley, a student of literary history, argued, "Why ban a book?" and cited LOTR, Catcher, and the Bible as part of the Eckhart curriculum to justify his enlightened philosophy of literature.

"You're right, Mr. O'Malley. Why ban a book? If you don't like it, don't read it, but don't try to suppress it. The Founders stressed freedom of press for a reason. They knew it would foster the best kind of society—the well read society." I responded seconds before I noticed my Father's big, red truck rolling through the evergreen Eckhart entrance.

I hopped into his Hinder Ford, he told me how much he and my mother were worried about me, and authoritatively informed me that I was not allowed to go to school this semester. I requested to be allowed to attend school, but he refused, and put me under house arrest like Galileo—who protested the Catholic Church by proposing a theory incongruous with their worldview, had been 500 years earlier.

Shrine of the Little Flower Cathedral. Georgetown University. August 25th, 2004.

"How long has it been since your last confession?" Father Michael asked a sun baked college freshmen.

"Oh, I'm not Catholic. I'm a Southern Baptist. Although I probably could use a confession—I haven't exactly been a saint recently. I still try to follow the Golden Rule in every thing though. And that's the most important thing I think. But I'm coming to you because I'd like to help out my friend and don't know how. He's Catholic and right now he's in some serious trouble. He's struggling with a lot of issues of faith and of mind. A friend of mine that has known him since was six said he may be suffering from a mental illness. He also has trouble accepting the teachings of his Catholic faith. I was hoping you could give me some counsel so I can maybe talk to him and pray for him." Mary replied.

"The House of the Lord is open to all. So I'd be glad to help, young lady. What kind of issues he is dealing with?" Father Michael inquired.

"Well, he's trying to find a new way to God and can't accept any one else as an authority. He stays up all night, searching for answers but when he opens his mouth a lot of what he says sounds bizarre. But he's such a great guy, Father. He's very faithful and tries his best to serve others. I think if he was from an older generation he could have easily been a priest. He's also really innocent sexually and was surrounded by a lot of sex this summer. I think that got to him. But now, I'm really worried about him. He's throwing away his future by being such a nonconformist. He got arrested twice this summer—not for anything immoral, but for behaving outlandishly. I just want the best for him and could really use the help of a spiritual intermediary." Mary responded.

"Well, from what you're telling me about him, what's his name?" Father Michael asked.

"Christopher" Mary answered.

"Well, from what you're telling me it sounds like Christopher, despite his eccentricities, is a man of God. That's the most important thing and a blessing. To quote the Sacred Scripture, "Blessed is the man that walks not in the counsel of the ungodly, nor stands in the way of sinners, nor sits in the seat of the scornful. But his delight is in the law of the Lord; and in his law he mediates day and night."

If your friend keeps mediating on the law of the Lord day and night, I have faith that his findings will allow him to triumph over whatever troubles the world brings him. Spiritual truth is a foundation of rock and will ground his life in the right until the end.

Now, it seems like the troubles he's experiencing are of the contemporary world. The Good News is that these troubles are merely temporary. There's a lot of darkness in this world and it's understandable that it would be hard for him to find the light of the Lord in such a place. The best you can do, in my judgment, is to pray unceasingly that he keeps searching until he finds that light. Because with that light comes understanding and with that understanding comes peace, which is what he needs the most right now. Peace. May the Peace of the Lord be with you and may it be with Christopher. Let us pray." Father Michael told Mary.

"May the peace of the Lord our God be with Christopher as he makes his way through this time of darkness to the eternal light of the Father, we pray. In the name of the Father, and of the Son, and of the Holy Spirit, Amen. Pray with your heart, young lady and the Lord will answer. Go in peace. God bless you. Chris is very lucky to have a friend like you." Father Michael followed.

"Thank you, Father." Mary responded.

Bel Air, MD. August 26, 2004.

Three silent nights after my house arrest began, my parents informed me that we were going on a "trip" to Baltimore to talk to "someone who would help me sleep". I really didn't object because I turned to my deeply religious reserves, writing off the trip as part of God's plan. I wasn't necessarily wrong despite my cloudy condition. Furthermore, the prospect of a sleep-aid seemed like a divinely sanctioned act of mercy. So as I entered my parent's car for what would inevitably be my final car ride as a preacher on drugs, put on my headphones and tuned out to the band I had fallen in love with in the Beginning—The Counting Crows, I said not a word of protest.

The music of the Counting Crows just had such a therapeutic feel to it and that's why, under the blanket of stars that graced the Baltimore night sky, I just let it soothe my suffering soul. Duritz's poetic words filled me with so much joy and the song, "I'm not sleeping anymore" certainly provided empathy. Since mid-July I had been a devout insomniac. It was late August now. August 26th in fact, forty days after the flight began.

As we reached Baltimore City, thirty three minutes after we quietly departed Bel Air, the song "Miller's Angels" radiated through my headphones. Miller's Angels, was a song with an interesting poetic conception—what if there were really angels, but they weren't all benevolent—like angels that bring you to the high poles for a momentary glimpse of heaven only to bring you down to the low poles for a much longer taste of Hell. Like the angels that trigger my soon to be diagnosed source of racing thoughts, scattered speech, and grandiose ideation.

Sleep

"A good laugh and a long sleep are the best cures in the doctor's book"
—Irish proverb

When we finally reached our destination, I was too deeply absorbed in the therapeutic tunes that thundered from my I-pod to tune into the sober present, which was less than Romantic. It was a sober present grounded on the hard, empirical fact that I was headed to an appointment with a mental health expert. Quite simply, in my artistically conceived awareness, the pending psychoanalysis session simply was not a concrete reality. Furthermore, my parents told me that I was meeting with "someone who would help me sleep"—not with a Lebanese psychiatrist.

Therefore, when I walked wearily up the weathered stairs to see an office legitimized by Johns Hopkins alumni magazines, I failed to make a connection natural to the healthy observer—a connection between my Suess-character behavior and subsequent mission to a mental health professional. I just assumed, in light of my parent's previous commentary, that I was destined to converse with an authority that would cure my insomnia—not psychoanalyze me.

And so I just sat in the ominous office, chemically bound to the Counting Crows, oblivious to the oral exchanges that seesawed between my concerned parents and the attentive office owner in the next room. I was obviously, based upon my lack of cognitive understanding of the present, still plunged deeply in my mystical dive and, in accordance with my infant Protestant faith, categorically classified this experience as part of the surf on the Great Wave of Destiny.

"What changes have you seen in your son that have sparked this appointment?" Dr. Nasabi asked the Castiles.

"All of a sudden, Christopher started talking really deeply about religion in all of these metaphors. His thoughts were really grandiose and when he talked his ideas were all over the place. Something wasn't right with him. But we thought he was just doing drugs. But as the behavior kept repeating itself no matter where our son was, down the beach, at home, at concerts, we thought it might be more complicated than drugs. Something was different about him. We'd like you to help us find out what it is." Mrs. Castile answered.

"Have the changes led to any adverse consequences?" Dr. Nasabi followed.

"Yes, our son got arrested twice this summer. Not for anything immoral, he's a good kid, but for behaving impulsively. On one occasion he interrupted cops while they wrote alcohol citations and on another for lying on the street imitating Gandhi. Also, he went to an alumni function at Eckhart and left his car doors open. The police were called." Mrs. Castile answered.

"What changes have you seen, dad?" Dr. Nasabi asked Mr. Castile.

"My son just talks and acts like a hippie now. Instead of lying around philosophizing, I'd like to see him working hard in the classroom, staying active, and concentrating on his studies." Mr. Castile answered.

"How bout you grandma?" Dr. Nasabi asked Mrs. Floyd, Mrs. Castile's mother.

"He just doesn't seem like the grandson I've known for the last nineteen years." Mrs. Floyd answered.

Three minutes after my parents and grandmother were called in, the doctor—a small, Middle Eastern man in his early seventies, emerged from his office wearing a face normally reserved for funerals saying, "I'd like to speak with *him,* now," in a graveyard tone.

Honestly, as I said in an earlier version of this story's intro, I couldn't relate to this man—the pictures of the world that we had embedded in our heads, to use a concept introduced to me by a former professor, were too diverse. Dr. Nasabi's was a black and white Roman Catholic photograph.

It was composed of dichotomies like heaven/hell, saints/sinners, good/evil and had concretely defined images of acceptable and unacceptable behavior, belief structure, and epistemological (knowledge theory) understandings of the world. Mine however, was a tie-died mural with all of the world's great culturally constructed faiths an integral part.

The lines between acceptable and unacceptable behavior thus were slightly blurred, the belief structures were more like enlightened guides, and the epistemological understandings weighed heavily upon the mind's creative faculties. Additionally, I was flying in Plato's form world at this point in my life as a result of the serotonin-spun summer and he was laboring in Aristotle's hard, objective world as a result of years of medical practice. A crash collision of worldview was inevitable.

After I reluctantly turned off my I-pod and meekly tip-toed into the plaque filled office, Dr. Nasabi quickly asked me the ultimate question—one that plucked away at my soul's most sensitive nerves and boiled my Polish blood especially because of what it suggested. It was an unfair question because its answer simply could not have been expressed using language due to its Beyond Words nature. In addition to being an inquiry that made me want to scream like the guy in that classic Norwegian painting, it also brought me down to the concrete reality that his man was a mental health professional.

"What has happened since Meister Eckhart?" Dr. Nasabi inquired.

I should have just ignored that question and stayed silent. This man was a stranger and I really didn't feel like articulating a book's worth of experience to him in one moment. However, I tried in my irrational state to answer the psychoanalytic query. By doing so, I manifested the classic signs reflective of people with my condition.

My speech was jumpy and unorganized due to the thoughts that raced through my brain. My ideas bounced from one unrelated idea to the other. And once again I started act like a character from a Dr. Suess story. Clearly the bad brain chemistry that my condition had been brewing sizzled whatever streaks of Reason I once held firmly.

After my broken answer, which I turned into a haphazardly arranged joke, "Well a lot has happened since Eckhart, doctor. What hasn't happened since Eckhart? What I have to say is that I have a six sense—

a sense of humor and I want to tell the world that sound of an improvised fart is humorous," the doctor called my parents and my grandmother back into the office.

Upon my trinity's arrival, I began to release all of the bottled up anger that I had stored from the summer on the classic Oedipal target—my Father, who art not in heaven, like Jesus' Father, but at my side in a therapist's office.

"Dad, you want them to take me away?" I yelled ferociously at my Father, critical of his objectives for shipping me to the Catholic therapist. His objectives were, as I failed to realize at the time, rooted in compassion and my best interest.

Instinctively, the doctor, as he cautiously took notes chimed in, "I don't think the House is right for you, but if you start behaving like this in front of the Judge he could order an evaluation and you could be sent there!"

His caution however, registered no concern in my battle-tested Soul. I wasn't worried about the Judge for one, because I was so intensely focused on the present moment due to its severity. For two, I wasn't worried about the Judge because I had such unshakable faith that my arresting officer would "talk to the Judge for me" as he said he would and facilitate the administration of Justice. And for three, because I was smart enough not to mouth off to a Judge. Psychiatry is very theoretical and has many different schools—Freudian, Jungian, Logotherapeutic, to name a few. Justice however, is blind.

Dr. Nasabi then described my symptoms—racing thoughts, disorganized and hurried speech, unrealistic belief in ones abilities before finally conceding, "Fortunately I know what it is and I know how to treat it," as my parents sighed in relief and I grew emotional.

The last forty days in the mystic rave, although wild, were easily the scariest of my life. I couldn't sleep, I couldn't think clearly, and I ended up, as a result, with a bounty of scar tissue and piercing memories.

"Your child has **Bipolar Disorder,**" Nasabi followed. "Millions of Americans suffer from it. We're not sure exactly what triggers it, but we know genetics and environment play a significant role."

This diagnosis shouldn't have been a surprise to my parents. Days after the Counting Crows incident, my former journalism teacher suggested the diagnosis to them after a phone conversation with me. His best friend in college had similar symptoms because he had the same condition. So my teacher, a very brilliant man, was able to pin down the diagnosis with ease despite a lack of advanced training in psychology and medicine. Additionally, **BPD** ran in my father's bloodline—both of his brothers had it.

It was a surprise to me though to learn that there was a less than supernatural reason for my frenzied thought, speech, and insight. I thought God gave me a mission. Perhaps this assessment still was accurate but maybe my mission was to tell this story so it could help others rather than to start a national revolution in religious consciousness. Although maybe such a revolution where "Golden Rule, God is Love" Spirituality replaces "Jesus died for your sins and hates gay people" Religion would be in America's best interest.

Regardless, now severed from Mary, from Elizabeth—from any female contact, in a shrink's office while filtering the threat of hospitalization, I began to finally let the sad, sad, tears pour down my face. I was lucky to have good parents, but I didn't have a girl-only a mental illness. And when that hard fact hit me and made me fully conscious of my current state as a mentally ill loser—a Noah's flood of tears became the inevitable result.

Seeing my trauma and long overdue tears, Dr. Nasabi pulled out a little blue pill and dictated, "You must take this."

My parents looked over at me with glances suggesting I concede but I was hesitant. I couldn't help but recall, in this critical moment, a scene from the philosophical mindbender—the Matrix. In that rich, complex film, the movies protagonist—Neo, is offered a pill by the older, wiser Morpheus and it instantly alters his perception of "reality".

"My faith won't let me take that pill." I told the doctor in a teary tone, skeptical of the Science behind it. I genuinely believed that I had experienced the world as I had for a reason so I stubbornly refused the pill's medical wonder. My faith was uniquely Protestant.

However, it was overridden by a faith that was commonly Catholic—the faith of the therapist who told me that it was because of his faith that he worked seventy hours a week, thereby exhibiting the classical distinction between Catholicism and Protestantism. The Catholic formula for salvation is faith + good works + sacramental rites. The Protestant formula is faith + grace alone. Your salvation is not contingent upon your action in Protestantism. It is in Catholicism however. Consequently, medical expertise and active faith on his side, Dr. Nasabi urged me to take the pill for my own good.

I stalled in contemplation for a few moments, as everyone grew intensely anxious, until Intervention. The celestial sound of a benevolent angel rung through my ears and set off the last "aha" moment of insight.

I now realized that this pill too was part of God's plan—that it symbolized the crashing of the great Wave and the peace to follow. If I wanted to be Catholic, I could have just trusted the doctor's word that it would be in my best interest to take the pill and save myself from abstraction. But for this forty day rave, as you could probably tell, I was on a vacation from Catholicism. I would return to the faith, but not until hearing the beautiful sermons of the late Father Philip DiChico and growing in Love and consequently Wisdom.

And so, under the influence of my guardian angel—the same angel that I prayed to every single night before sleep when I was a little boy, the same angel that comforted me in all my childhood dreams, the same angel that protected my bright little soul from the forces of darkness, I finally accepted my fate and took the little blue pill. Quickly, I felt my brain chemistry change and lull me into a comfortably medicated state.

The sensation of a blue psychoactive balancing my high levels of serotonin created one of those Zen "ah" moments because it symbolically sang a requiem for the nightmare of not having a cure for an unkind condition. It also ushered in the funeral for my frenzy of confusion and sleepless nights. But most of all, however, it gave birth to the Genesis of a new found faith in friends and family.

I was a freshmen philosophy major and got too caught up in conjectures—ontological arguments, metaphysical systems, cosmological arguments, for the existence of God to see ultimately, the God was love and his presence ran through friends and family more than anything.

In the sublime connections of family, friends, and the rest of his Creation, as I finally discovered when the Great Wave crashed and I stared out into the rising Sun from the beach sands, this is where we'll find God—the unwavering Presence of Love, *hiding*. If of course, we'd only wake up from our socially-conditioned slumbers, stop speculating his whereabouts in the clouds with our blind eyes, and simply go out and *seek* him on the earth as guided by the light of our open hearts.

"God is love and he who abides in God abides in love, and God in him."

I recited silently in the office of psychiatry, memories of my Catholic Confirmation Mass now resurrected.

"I guess my friends and family deserve an apology. I feel like a jackass now. I can't believe I didn't realize this stuff earlier. God is love and runs through friends and family more abundantly than anything. I like that. Oh well, at least I finally learned it. At least the wave finally crashed. Better late than never." I concluded in silence.

"In the old days, he would have been in the house." Nasabi interrupted with an eerie echo of expired truth.

"Well, I don't know if you read the news today, but it's 2000 and four. It's the new days bitch. And you *just* said that you didn't think the house was right for me. Flip/Flop. Flip/Flop." I snapped back.

"Plus, if they had homes for sane today, they'd all be empty because no real person can engage this insane world and completely preserve their mental health." My mother interjected.

"Yeah. This isn't a curse. Being just a little crazy is necessary for our survival. Because it's like Seal said, "But we are never gonna survive unless we get a little crazy."

"Seal, who is that? I've never heard of a Seal. Must be a young people thing." Nasabi answered.

"He's only a staple of mid-90's popular culture. Never heard "Kissed by a Rose" or "Fly like an Eagle"? I can't believe you've never heard of Seal." I followed. "He rocks."

"I don't listen to music. I don't believe in it. And you need to learn to respect your elders." Nasabi responded.

"That makes sense that you would say that because Missy Elliot was right—Music make you lose control. Therapists like control. Kids like music. So I can see why you don't like music. It make kids lose control. But as far as respect for elders go, I have it. Just not for one's that say "in the old days, he would have been in the house" like I'm not in the room and is if that statement were relative to the present—just not for one's that think they're better than me because they have some fancy degree. It will be a better world when the power of love conquers the love of power, doctor."

"The bill is $150. I accept cash or check." Nasabi answered.

"Wow that's a pretty lucrative faith there, doctor. Seventy hours a week plus $150 an hour equals…10, 000 dollars a week! 10,000 dollars a week plus fifty two weeks." I replied.

"Chris, enough. Here's your check doctor." My Father answered.

"I'd like to see him regularly for the next month. A period of severe depression usually follows mania." Nasabi told my parents.

"Wow that's over 400 g's a year! I wanna be a psychiatrist!" I yelled.

"We'll see doctor. I'm not sure if you're right for us." My mother responded and we left the mental health office as a family.

"Somebody needs to tell that guy that everybody farts. What a hardass. Please never let me take myself that seriously." I told my parents as my Father started the car.

"I know, ever heard of laughter?" My mother said as we made our way out of the parking lot.

"Ever heard of humility?" My grandmother said as we pulled up to a red light.

"Well I haven't heard of a good sleep in a long time." I replied.

"When we get home you can get some, baby cakes. The medicine should help." My mother answered.

"Ok mom, but don't call me baby cakes. I'm a man now." I responded.

"True," said my mother, "but you're also a virgin."

The light turned green and we headed back to the Garden, leaving behind the looniest bin, never to forget, even in life's darkest moments, the sixth sense of humor that lies within.

"Nice burn mom. I guess I know where I get my crazy gene from" was all that was said on the way before my parent's sun baked smiles signaled a long overdue amen and my heavy snores sang the requiem for the nightmare of an insomnia that seemed would go without end.

August and Everything After

"Smooth seas do not make skillful sailors"—African Proverb

After I said goodbye to Saturn, the next few years would be spent returning to Earth. I had gone on an extraordinary voyage of discovery, but now found myself far away from home.

After receiving proper medication and diagnosis, I was able to sleep regularly. This was a blessing. But when I reflected on what had happened while I was "manic" as I came down—getting arrested twice, embarrassing myself constantly, quitting my job, withdrawing from college, I became extremely depressed. For the sake of decency, I won't go into too much detail about the experience but I will say that for as I high as I was at points in this story, I was just as low at points in the next two years to follow.

I made myself believe that I was "mentally ill" and in need of constant therapy and condescension, so I let my will to live die out. "Oh, you're crazy you'll never amount to anything" I kept telling myself. "You're another BPD looney, why go on" was a mantra I couldn't rid my psyche of. As evident by these thoughts, I had found myself, shortly after coming down from the high pole of mania, down to the low pole of depression. And I was in hell.

I used to be religious but was indoctrinated by an expert to believe that my powerful experiences were merely illusory. A former class clown and handsome soccer player, I was now a joke. Fat, drunk, and stupid. Lazy and unlovable. A real loser I was in my mind, out of touch with reality. Mentally ill. Unworthy of respect, unworthy of dignity—unworthy of life. The fact that my youth was blissful only added to the pain. Truly, when you've experienced the highest pinnacles of heaven—the lowest depths of hell are infinitely hotter. I tried to find comfort in food and ended up gaining seventy pounds. I now found myself a 275 pound bipolar loser without the will to keep living, just three years after being one of the happiest Seniors at Eckhart.

In a desperate act of a dying hope for salvation from the psychological suffering, I began to start taking some baby steps in the positive direction. At first I simply began to record my thoughts and attend Catholic mass—both actions helped instrumentally to my full recovery. Recording my thoughts—recounting my memories served the therapeutic function of releasing my stored frustration with my manic/depressive life. Attending masses led by Father Phil not only started to heal my soul but also guided me to a deeper Wisdom.

Although the process took around two and half years inevitably I was able to step by step, resurrect myself from deep depression to authentic happiness. Part of the reason, as I previously stated, was attending Catholic mass, and literary therapy but another—a key factor in the later stages of the recovery-so, so mood to legitimate happiness, besides some Grace, was my discovery of some life-shaping philosophies. Some of the aphorisms they contained were very instrumental in my gradual climb to authentic happiness.

"It's not the things themselves that disturb men, but their judgments about them"
–Stoicism

"If you don't compete or compare and simply be yourself everyone will respect you"
–Daoism

"If you bring forth what is within you, what you bring forth will save you."
–Gnosticism

Reflecting on my forty day rave, these strong philosophies as my light, I began to change my mind about my condition.

Of course I suffered, but suffering when survived only builds character. Of course I had been out of my body, but in Ancient Greece—the most intellectually advanced culture in history, such a state was praised and respected as being a state in which an individual transcends ordinary consciousness and has a heightened capacity for exceptional thought and experience as a result. Of course I had a condition that I would have to take medication for the rest of my life to neutralize but at least there existed the medication to treat it. Of course I had experienced girl problems, but what teenage male hasn't. And at least I came away from them with a loyal female friend.

Of course I had Bipolar Disorder, but so have a lot of smart, creative people in history. The fact that I had it put me in company with amazing artists such as: Vincent Van Gogh, F Scott Fitzgerald, Ralph Waldo Emerson, Jimi Hendrix, Edgar Allen Poe, Beethoven, Mozart, and Mark Twain among others.

The biggest fruit of my fair assessment of my condition however, was the complete realization that I was no longer mentally ill. Happy, creative, medicated, educated, and slightly enlightened, I was instead "mentally chill". And that discovery, my friends, metaphorically double banked Socially Held Stereotypes' last cup giving me the Win, in case you are not familiar with the rules of Ruit, without *any* chance for rebuttal.

May God love you,

Christopher Castile
Sacred Heart University
December 16, 2006.

Printed in the United States
77870LV00002B/373-471

9 781424 171026